9/11

The Faerie Locket

Don't Miss These Other
Practical Guide Companion Novels

Monster Slayers
Lukas Ritter

Aldwyns Academy
Nathan Meyer

Nocturne
L.D. Harkrader

The Faerie Locket

Susan J. Morris

BOOKS FOR
YOUNG READERS

The Faerie Locket

©2011 Wizards of the Coast LLC

Published by Wizards of the Coast LLC

DUNGEONS & DRAGONS, WIZARDS OF THE COAST, and their respective logos are trademarks of Wizards of the Coast LLC in the U.S.A. and other countries.

Printed in the U.S.A.

Cover art by Emily Fiegenschuh
First Printing: March 2011

9 8 7 6 5 4 3 2 1

ISBN: 978-0-7869-5562-6
ISBN: 978-0-7869-5883-2 (e-book)
620-21103000 -001-EN

Library of Congress Cataloging-in-Publication Data
Morris, Susan J.
  The faerie locket / Susan J. Morris.
    p. cm.
   ISBN 978-0-7869-5562-6
  [1. Fantasy. 2. Magic--Fiction. 3. Fairies--Fiction. 4.
Sisters--Fiction.] I. Title.
  PZ7.M82875Fae 2011
  [Fic]--dc22

                                              2010032320

U.S., CANADA,
ASIA, PACIFIC, & LATIN AMERICA
Wizards of the Coast LLC
P.O. Box 707
Renton, WA 98057-0707
+1-800-324-6496

EUROPEAN HEADQUARTERS
Hasbro UK Ltd
Caswell Way
Newport, Gwent NP9 0YH
GREAT BRITAIN
Please keep this address for your records.

Visit our Web site at www.dungeonsanddragons.com

10 11 12 13 14 15 16   QG-FF

For Axel, who taught me the meaning of unconditional love.

Prologue

Vira Wyvernsting and Jade Farstar pressed themselves against the icy walls of a crevasse in the Dragonsmaw Cave. Their chests heaved as they struggled to keep their breathing quiet. Vira Wyvernsting cocked a slender, upswept ear for sound of pursuit.

But it didn't take the uncanny senses of an elf to hear the snuffling just outside their hiding place or to see the large foot—tipped with claws as big as Jade Farstar—press into the ice just outside. Then, another foot passed, and the long tail, which scraped along the ground with a hiss.

"We can't beat it," Jade Farstar whispered when the creature continued down the far passage.

"The villagers are depending on us," Vira Wyvernsting said, looking up at the pixie, barely the size of one of her ears. "Don't give up yet. We may be too small to beat it in a contest of arms, but we can still outsmart it. White dragons are notoriously dumb. We'll lure it into the back portion of its cave, pretending to be too weak and confused to continue fighting. Then, when it's right where we want it, we'll trigger a cave-in, trapping it!"

"That's a brilliant idea!" Jade Farstar said, a little too loudly. Her voice echoed off the icy walls, and she clapped her hands over her mouth, but it was too late. The dragon snorted, and a humongous, yellow-red eye appeared outside the crevasse.

"Or we could run!" Jade Farstar said. Her wings buzzed as she launched herself into the air.

"Quick! To the back of the cave!" Vira Wyvernsting said. "We can still do this!"

The dragon screeched at its discovery, and wicked, cold claws came grasping after them as they darted out from the crevasse, racing for the back of the cavern. The dragon's footsteps boomed behind them like orc drums of war. Then Jade Farstar heard the long, raspy intake of breath—the tell-tale sign of a dragon about to unleash its ultimate weapon.

"Oh no!" Jade Farstar cried. "It's going to breathe!"

Jade Farstar and Vira Wyvernsting dived for cover, screaming . . .

Chapter One

Jade woke to the scream of a tea kettle. She blinked, lost for a minute. Light filtered through the sheets strung up around her lower bunk. Ceramic cups clanged, and the tea kettle quieted.

She couldn't even remember having fallen asleep. When had that happened? And moreover, *what* had happened? Did Jade Farstar and Vira Wyvernsting succeed, or had the white dragon managed to escape the icy cave-in and destroy the village below?

Shedding her blankets, she parted the sheets that transformed her lower bunk into the Dragonsmaw Cave and stepped out onto the floor.

Daylight painted the loft in shades of pumpkin and gold. The round candle she'd held last night had burned down to a thumb-sized nub and lay on her bedside table. Beside it, hanging on a tarnished candelabra, was a sunny paper crown.

Jade grinned and swept up the crown and squashed

it on her head, hiding the tangled mass of her dandelion yellow hair.

Today was her twelfth birthday. It was going to be the best birthday ever. She could feel it.

She glanced up at the top bunk, but to her disappointment, it was empty, as was usual these days. Still, she had hoped her birthday might be different. Her sister, Vira, was learning to be a ranger, something that required getting up in the early light of dawn.

Learning to be a ranger meant Vira was gone all the time, even on important days like today. It had been hard to adjust at first. But Vira had the chance to learn to be just like her character Vira Wyvernsting, from her stories, and Jade couldn't begrudge her that. She'd jump at the chance to be the real Jade Farstar. But then, Jade would have to grow up to be a pixie—or, considering the height of pixies, grow down?—and the chances of that were slim. Or so she'd been told by her teacher. Instead, her teacher said, she should focus her energy on wizardry school. As if human magic were better than faerie magic.

Her teacher simply didn't understand. Jade just couldn't help but wish she could live in the world of her older sister's stories. They felt so real, so much more vivid than the tiny human village in which she lived. More than anything, she wanted to find a door into that other world. There, she could go on adventures with the faeries, elves, and fey creatures that lived in Golden Leaf forest and forget about chores, about being respectable, and about how her sister had less and less time for her.

It used to be that whenever their chores were done, and sometimes, even when they weren't, Vira and Jade would sneak out into the woods into the old tree house to tell stories, or, when it was too dark or cold for that, they'd crawl under the covers of the Dragonsmaw Cave, like they did last night. But lately, Vira had gotten busier and busier and no longer had as much time to tell Jade tales of Golden Leaf.

The enticing aroma of freshly baked bread wrapped around Jade like a blanket when she reached the top of the stairs. She was suddenly ravenous. She descended into the kitchen.

"The dragon emerges!" her mother said as Jade plopped down at the table. Jade smiled as her mother swept by, pecking a kiss on her forehead. "Breakfast is on the table—biscuits with honey and fresh milk from the cow. I've got to go to the market. Catch you later, pumpkin!" Then, with a swirl of blue cloth, her mother was out the door.

Jade blinked. Her mother hadn't even noticed the birthday crown on her head or told her to wash her hands. She supposed her mother was busy, but still. She heard a happy yowl, and Fluffy, the family's ugly orange tomcat, pounced onto her lap.

Her family wouldn't just forget her birthday, would they? No, of course they wouldn't, she reassured herself, petting Fluffy somewhat harder than was strictly necessary. They must still be getting ready. It was the only thing that made sense. Fluffy meowed and dug his claws in.

Well, if her family wasn't around to celebrate her birthday, then they weren't around to tell her she couldn't have a picnic breakfast up in the tree house either. And that, followed by curling up with a good book, sounded like a wonderful way to spend the morning. The purring abruptly stopped as she jumped up, dumping Fluffy to the floor.

Jade grabbed a couple of biscuits coated in honey—one for the faeries and one for her—wrapped them up in one of the cloth napkins, and stuffed them in her pockets. Downing a glass of milk in one gulp and grabbing *A Practical Guide to Faeries*, a book about faeries her sister had lent her, she made for the tree house.

When Jade was five, her family had moved from the bustling city of Sunspire to the small, red-doored house on the edge of the Oakspring Forest. The very best part of living on the edge of the Oakspring Forest was the tree house they had found a stone's throw into the woods. And the very best part of the tree house was the faerie box they had found inside it.

It took nearly a year of badgering her mother to clear the ivy out of the tree house and to replace enough of the rotting wood to make it useable again. But after that, it had become the perfect place to escape and spend a lazy afternoon, reading, telling stories, or playing.

Sometimes, Jade liked to climb up there by herself and just watch the world go by. The sun would set and her family would hurry around, dryads would slip by like mist in the forest below, an owlbear cub would stop to scratch its stomach—and not one would look up and notice her there in the tree house window. And while she never caught sight of the faeries that must visit the faerie box, she could sometimes hear the dragons singing in the distant Widow's Teeth mountains.

Jade scrambled up the old oak, hand over practiced hand, her book in her teeth, and pulled herself up through the trapdoor in the floor of her tree house, then closed the door behind her.

Strangely, the faerie box had been in almost perfect condition the day they found it. She had discovered it, but her sister was the one who had figured out it was a faerie box. From then on, they left pieces of biscuit dipped in honey out every day for the faerie folk.

Sometimes, the faeries would leave things in the box for them in return—an acorn, a daisy chain, a smooth river stone. Jade would bring these items to Vira, and Vira would tell her the story of the artifacts from Golden Leaf. Then Jade would put them in a special pinewood box she had under her bed at home, and take them out at night and remember the magic that had brought them to her.

The faerie box, made of smooth wood that glittered silver and charcoal like a moth's wing, had a dark, thatched roof, and was attached to the wall of the tree house, opposite the window. Setting her book down, Jade brushed off the dust that had gathered on the wooden box, lifted the lid, and peered inside.

Nestled within was a glint of gold chain. She felt her heart skip a beat. This was bigger than anything the faeries had left them before.

Reaching in and lifting it out with the greatest of care so that it wouldn't catch on the rough edges of the box, she saw the chain belonged to a locket—one big enough to cover the palm of her hand. Carved out of the front, like a window into another world, was the silhouette of a birch leaf. A golden leaf locket.

Golden Leaf.

Jade felt her pulse quicken. A birthday present from the faeries themselves, with the emblem of Golden Leaf on it! She hugged it to her chest as though it might disappear at any moment. She couldn't think of anything she'd ever wanted more.

She tried to open it, but the lock was stuck. Disappointment pulled at her, but she quickly swallowed it. It wouldn't do to be ungrateful for such a brilliant gift.

The faeries might be upset and never leave her anything ever again, or may even take this one back. Besides, she consoled herself, her mother could surely fix something so small as a stuck locket once she showed it to her.

She shoved the locket in her pocket. Pulling out the napkin, she deposited one of the honey-encrusted biscuits inside the faerie box and closed the lid. Normally she just left some crumbs, but she felt that a more substantial offering was definitely in order after the lovely gift they'd left for her.

A chill breeze swept through the window, and laughter rang like silver bells behind her, approaching the tree house. Jade leaned out the window.

A group of strange, dark-haired girls was approaching her home. Jade squinted, trying to make out more details. Each of the girls stood taller than Vira. They were pale as the moon and as fine-boned as birds. Their hair was not simply dark—it was so black it seemed to swallow the light.

What were they doing coming to her house when no one was home? Should she do something? She could use the sling concealed somewhere in the tree, or she could run to the market and raise the alarm. Then she caught sight of Vira in the midst of them, talking and pointing, and smiled. Whoever they were, they were friends of Vira's.

Jade popped open the trapdoor and scrambled down the tree, eager to show Vira the present she had received from the faeries. She knew her sister would be impressed. Maybe Vira could open the locket where Jade had failed.

As she got closer, she noticed the girls' eyes were solid silver, and their ears were lobeless and ended in fine points. Elves, Jade realized with a thrill. Some of them dwelled in the Feywild, the magical world of the faeries, as well as in the world of the humans, though Jade couldn't imagine why anyone who had the option of living in the Feywild would ever want to live in the world of the humans.

The elves, with their long life spans, ethereal appearances, and supernatural gifts, tended to keep to themselves, leaving the small human settlement on the edge of the Oakspring Forest to its mundane existence. Jade hadn't seen elves since her family left Sunspire. What was Vira doing with them?

The elves turned around as one—such a fluid motion it made her gasp to watch—to look at something on the horizon, and she saw the insignia on each of their cloaks: the silver moon of the Moonsing Archers. A polished, bone white bow was slung over each girl's back. The same cloak and bow Vira had.

Why hadn't her sister told her she was training with elves? Elves were akin to faeries, and Jade was fascinated with faeries—Vira knew that. Jade couldn't stop a grin from slipping onto her face. Elves! Vira was training with the elves to become a ranger—her sister was closer than ever to actually being Vira Wyvernsting. And Jade was about to meet these elves.

"Vira!" Jade called, cupping her hands around her mouth. "Vira, wait!"

The procession stopped and the elves turned to fix her with those unsettling silver eyes. Jade hesitated. They were a little more intimidating than she remembered, and a lot more intimidating in person than on the pages of a book.

"Oh!" the nearest elf said, tilting her head. "You didn't tell us you had a baby sister." Jade felt the blood rush to her face. Not quite the greeting she had hoped for, but it wouldn't hold her back.

"Well met, I'm Jade," she said, and she stuck out her hand. She was satisfied to see that she trembled only a little bit and that, she told herself, was in anticipation. The elf looked down at Jade's hand, then looked at Vira.

Uh-oh. Did elves not shake hands? Had she just made some kind of etiquette mistake? She hadn't read anything about elves not shaking hands in Vira's book.

She looked at Vira. Vira studied their house most intently.

"She's . . . cute," the elf said. "What is she, eight?"

"Twelve today," Jade answered, dropping her hand to her side. "And I have a name." She winced as soon as she said it.

"And it's her birthday! How sweet." The elf once again

addressed Vira. Why wasn't Vira saying anything? "That would explain the crown. Why doesn't she come with us? We could always find a use for such a cute little girl."

Jade's heart beat faster. The elves wanted her to come along!

"Look, I know you're trying to be nice but "—Vira took a deep breath—"she's too little and inexperienced. She'd only slow us down."

"Slow you down!" Jade began. How exactly would she slow them down? All right, she was inexperienced, but she wasn't little—she was twelve today, to be exact.

"Jade, go home," Vira said.

"I am home!" Jade frowned. "And . . . I have to show you something. The faeries left me a birthday present." Why did she feel so childish saying the word "birthday"? Was there a more adult way to put it? "It's from Golden Leaf. Just like your stories!"

The elves looked Jade up and down as though she were some rare species of rodent. Jade fought the urge to stick her tongue out at them, but she managed—just barely—to restrain herself.

"Jade, you're embarrassing me," Vira said. "Look, tonight I'll come see whatever it is you want to show me and we can talk about it, and then we'll do whatever you want. I promise. Just please be good right now and go play by yourself."

"But Vira, it's my birthday . . ." Jade hated the whine that crept into her voice. "And what about Golden Leaf?"

"Gods, Jade!" Vira colored. "Look, I hate to be the one to have to tell you, but clearly Mom left whatever bead or trinket you found in your doll house. She thinks you're . . . I don't know . . . five or something. Happy now?"

"No," Jade whispered. But it all made a horrible kind of sense. Her mother always took such a positive interest in Vira's stories of Golden Leaf. Encouraged them, even. Jade didn't know what was worse: finding out she was an embarrassment to her sister or finding out that everyone but her had seemed to know that the stories about the faeries from Golden Leaf hadn't been true.

Jade shook her head. "It can't be true."

"All right," Vira said cruelly. "Let's say it was faeries. Why would faeries care about a spoiled little girl like you?"

"Hey, I'm not–" Jade started, but Vira just talked over her.

"It must be for me. You never do anything interesting. All you ever do is follow me around."

"That's not true!" Jade hugged her arms tighter around herself, as though the locket might escape from her skirt pocket. Anger made it hard for her to form coherent sentences. All she could think about was how wrong her sister was. "I am interesting." That was weak. She had to do

13

better. "I do things on my own!" That was better? What did that even mean?

Vira snorted. "I'm sorry I ever told you those stupid stories about Golden Leaf. Your teacher is right. It's no good for you. All it's done is make you act like a baby."

Jade had had about enough. "Yeah, well, you're the one who told me those stupid stories," she shot back, gratified to see her sister's face tighten. "You think you're so special, like you're better than me, but you're just spoiled, and stuck-up, and a terrible sister!" Her sister's face went hard and Jade could have sworn she could see her own breath cloud in the air, it had gotten so cold.

Vira said something, but Jade couldn't hear her over the noise of her blood rushing in her ears. A painful, tingling sensation burned in her nose, and her vision blurred. She turned away so her sister and the elves wouldn't see.

"Gods," she heard one of the elves say in that musical voice. "What a baby." And that's when she began to run.

Tinkling laughter chased her all the way back to the tree house. She climbed the tree by memory, blinking back tears. Why did she have to cry? Crying always made people take her less seriously, as though she really were a baby, just like the elves had said.

She tore the locket from her pocket and took one look at it, its antique gold glittering in the morning light. It probably cost her mother two coppers at the local market.

Scowling, she threw it out the window and watched as it soared, then bounced off a tree, and fell to the forest below.

What a terrible birthday.

Chapter Two

The chiming of tiny bells caused Jade to turn around. The floor by the faerie box, strangely, glistened in the sunlight, like the slime from a snail's trail.

Jade sniffed angrily and rubbed her eyes clear. The elf's voice echoed in her head: *what a baby*. But when she opened her eyes, the floor still glittered. There were colors too, glowing emerald and swirling like smoke.

That was strange. What could cause . . .

The wood trembled and buckled beneath her, and Jade scrambled back as a chain of hard-nosed, red and white mushrooms burst through the floor.

The chiming grew louder, and green specks spun above the mushroom circle like fireflies, faster and faster, brighter and brighter, until they exploded in a shower of emerald light, filling the tree house with the sudden, intense smell of apples and freshly shorn grass.

A small, winged creature no bigger than her hand shot out of the light, bounced off the wall with a spray of golden dust and shattering ice, shook itself, then flew straight at her.

Jade covered her face with her arms and shrieked, but the creature didn't hit her. Instead, it hovered in front of her crossed arms, held aloft by two pairs of furiously buzzing dragonfly wings rimmed in frost.

The creature was a perfect miniature figure. Fingers, toes, mouth—all so small they could belong to a doll. But this little being had pointed ears and a spray of bright pink hair shot through with green spikes, and it could fly. A faerie! Jade's heart leaped into her throat. A pixie, to be exact, if the book her sister lent her could be believed.

"Did you find the locket?" the faerie said. It sounded exactly as Jade expected it to—magical, like the tinkling of bells and birdsong.

"I knew it!" Jade exclaimed, a thrill running through her. "Faeries did leave the locket." Boy, would Vira be surprised when she found out—if Jade decided to tell her, she thought with a little smile.

"The Sun Prince said it would be too difficult, and Quinn didn't think I could do it, and once the redcaps showed up and I had to send the locket to you through the faerie box, even I was worried that I couldn't do it, but you did, and I did, and it all worked out!" the faerie said in one breath, not waiting for an answer. The faerie glanced behind her at the mushroom circle. The green sparks had begun to brighten and swirl again. "Wait—you did find the locket, didn't you? I was only supposed to give it to Vira Wyvernsting. No one else. Just you, Vira."

Vira Wyvernsting? Her sister's character—the one from the stories. Jade's heart fell. Right. Of course it was her sister. She felt like crying all over again. No one, not even the faeries, wanted her.

"I'm not . . ." Jade began to confess, then stopped.

The faerie darted around the tree house like a bee on fire, lifting the lid of the faerie box, ducking into cubby holes, and checking under the piles of dried leaves on the floor. "Where is it?" the faerie cried. "That locket was very important, entrusted to me by the Sun King himself, and he didn't even want to have to trust a pixie, but he had to, because only a pixie had a chance at getting to you unnoticed and before the others, and I told him it would be all right, and the redcaps . . ."

Jade scrambled to her feet. Vira had made it pretty clear she thought all this Golden Leaf stuff was beneath her. And even if she hadn't, Vira wasn't here right now. There was no one else to help the faerie—it was up to Jade.

"The locket's outside!" Jade said. The faerie looked stricken. "Don't worry," Jade said quickly. "I'll get it." She wouldn't fail the faerie.

"Quickly! They're right behind me!" the faerie urged. "We can't let them find it."

"Wait, there are more of you?" Jade said.

Just then, there was a series of thuds followed by bright emerald flashes, like sheet lightning in the summer. One by one, seven ugly, crooked old men almost as tall as Jade exploded into the room. Each of the awful little men had a red cap and wore giant iron boots that left smoldering black marks on the oak floor.

Every one of Jade's muscles froze. Redcaps! Some of the foulest faeries the Feywild had to offer, according to her book, and servants of the dark Ice Queen herself.

"You get the locket!" the pixie said. "I'll hold them off!" The pixie flew like a stone out of a sling, straight at the nose of the nearest redcap. Jade watched, horrified, as it looked like the redcap was going to catch the faerie with his grimy claws, but the pixie escaped, diving through the evil old man's grasping fingers and putting on an extra burst of speed. "What are you waiting for? Go!" the pixie urged. "I can't do this all day!"

Jade forced herself to look away. She dashed over to the trapdoor, flung it open, and half fell, half climbed down the tree. The elves' bell-like voices rang in the distance, and she had the fleeting impulse to run and get her sister after all. This was too much for her. Her sister was right—the locket was intended for Vira. Her sister was the strong one, the brave one, and the one with any actual fighting skills.

Jade heard a high-pitched shriek from above, and she dived into the undergrowth, searching the ferns under the trees.

Where was that locket? It had to be here somewhere! Jade glanced up at the tree across from the tree house window—she remembered it bouncing off the trunk.

There! A chunk of bark was missing halfway down the tree. And if the locket had hit the tree there, then it should have fallen over in the rosebushes. She had been searching in the wrong spot. Cursing herself for being thickheaded—her sister wouldn't have made that mistake—she ran over to the rosebushes. At the base, tangled amid the thorns, was the locket.

Wincing as the sharp thorns drew across her skin, she grasped at the chain and pulled. The locket caught on a tangled branch. More flashes of light, and the sound of wood cracking and breaking came from above. Come on . . . Tugging harder, she pulled the locket up the branch. Thorns scratched her arms and cheek, and the branch bent but didn't give.

Come *on*!

She tumbled backward, the locket chain clutched in her hands.

"I've got it!" Jade called up to the faerie, waving the locket above her head. The faerie darted out the window and flew down to where she sat in the flowers.

"Oh thank goodness! You really had me worried there for a moment," the faerie said. "If you had lost the locket . . ."

"If *I* had lost the locket!" Jade protested.

"If *we* had lost the locket . . ." the faerie began. "But that doesn't matter now because you didn't!" And they grinned for a moment, their faces reflected in the golden locket.

Then, all seven redcaps leaped out of the window and landed at the base of the tree, sending dust and leaves swirling. Smoke rose from their iron boots, and the flowers and grass died where they stepped. The redcaps took one look at Jade and saw the locket, which was now glittering with unearthly light. They forgot about the pixie.

"Now what?" Jade backed away as the redcaps advanced, testing their scythes on the flora around them.

"I don't know," the pixie squeaked. "This is as far ahead as I thought!"

"Getting chased by redcaps is as far as you thought?" Jade exclaimed as the redcaps let out an unearthly howl. "That doesn't seem like a very good plan!"

The redcaps charged her as one. Stuffing the locket in her pocket, she dashed farther into the woods, the redcaps close on her heels. The faerie let out a squeal and followed.

"See, this is exactly the kind of thing the Sun King was talking about when he said he was worried I couldn't do it," the faerie said, buzzing by her ear. " 'Pixies don't think ahead,' he said. 'Pixies are weak,' he said. Why did I ever think I could do this? I'm such a bad Faerie Guide!"

"We need to get back to the tree house," Jade said, thinking quickly. Surely it could protect them from the redcaps until she and the pixie could figure out what to do.

"How?" the faerie said. "In case you hadn't noticed, we're going the wrong direction, and the redcaps are between us and the tree house!"

"I don't know," Jade said, starting to panic. The redcaps' breathing was almost as loud in her ears as her own. "Don't you have some faerie magic or something to distract them?"

"A distraction. Got it!" The pixie flew back into the faces of the redcaps, dropping a series of small balls that made loud banging sounds and released a bright light and a small puff of smoke. The redcaps stood dazed for a few precious heartbeats, then they reoriented and swatted at her, nearly clipping her wings. But the pixie flew out of reach.

"Hurry and do whatever you're going to do," the pixie cried, diving again to pitch another green ball at the redcaps. "I can't keep this up for very long!"

"All right, just get in the tree house. I've got this," Jade answered, hoping fervently it was true.

Taking advantage of the distraction the pixie gave her, Jade put some distance between herself and the redcaps. Now she tried to lead them farther away from the tree house and increase her lead on them at the same time, dodging trees and leaping bushes. She felt like a hero, hurtling through the woods.

But the redcaps were quicker than she expected, and soon, they were close on her heels again, their stale breath steaming on her neck. One of their yellowed claws swiped at her back. They were closing on her! How was she supposed to get away from them when they were every bit as fast as she was, if not faster?

Think, Jade, think! What would Jade Farstar do? Jade Farstar was clever, and while she wasn't always as strong or as big as her opponents—as a pixie, how could she be?—she always managed to use her agility and cleverness to outwit and outmaneuver them. She might not be Jade Farstar from the stories, but she was pretty agile, and the redcaps didn't seem to be the nimble, tree-climbing type.

Her eyes fell on a tree trunk. That was it!

Running hard at a large oak, she planted a foot firmly on it and pushed off, switching directions without losing a second of momentum. It felt like flying. She couldn't help but laugh.

The first redcap turned to watch her sail by for a heartbeat, a look of astonishment on his ugly face, before he ran headlong into the broad side of the same tree, followed by all six of his friends, one after the other.

Jade dashed toward the back side of the tree house.

Growls, yips, and snapping branches sounded behind her. The redcaps had regrouped and were chasing her once more, hopefully a little farther behind. She was too terrified to look. Reaching the tree house trunk, she climbed as she'd never climbed before, her heart pounding her in ears.

Just as her fingers closed around the edges of the trapdoor, she felt a cold, clammy hand with long, sharp nails catch at the edge of her skirt, then clamp down around her ankle.

No!

She looked down and saw the redcaps standing one on top of the other to reach her. Yelping, she struggled furiously, holding onto the top of the trapdoor with all her strength as the hand pulled her lower. The redcaps on the bottom of the pile reached their claws up at her, ready to grab her as soon as she came within reach. She could hear them cackling. "Pretty, pretty, pretty . . ."

Kicking down with her free leg, she caught her captor right in the nose. He let out a startled gurgle and fell off the tower of redcaps and into the rosebush below, pulling the other redcaps down with him.

The faerie swept open the trapdoor with a shower of emerald sparks, and Jade burst through. She barricaded the door with a bench from the corner of the tree house, then collapsed onto it, panting.

She made it.

"Put on the locket," the faerie said. "I have a hunch."

"A hunch?" Jade said. She couldn't believe what she was hearing. The trapdoor under Jade bumped and trembled. Jade glanced up at the faerie, her eyes wide. "You have a hunch? We're going to die in here!"

"Quickly! Before they break through!" the faerie said.

"All right, all right!" Jade said.

She pulled out the locket from her pocket. She paused a moment to stare—the locket hummed like a living thing and was warm to the touch—then quickly wrapped it around her neck.

She worked the clasp, but she couldn't quite get it to catch—her fingers had never felt so clumsy.

"We don't have time for this!" Jade said, watching, wide-eyed, as a sliver of steel traced its way around the edge of the trapdoor.

"Do you have a better idea?" the faerie said.

"Yes! We've got to get out of here," Jade said, running over to the window, her hands still trying to work the clasp. "Before it's too late." She could climb out the window, and the faerie could fly, and they could get higher than the piled-up redcaps could. That should keep them safe, at least for a little while.

"No, wait!" the faerie cried, flying around to Jade's back and pulling at the back of her shirt. "Trust me!"

Then all at once, the clasp caught. The cool, palm-sized

locket fell against her chest, the world stopped, and then, with an explosion of gold and green sparks, everything disappeared.

Chapter Three

The first thing Jade noticed was the sharp tang of apples—the same smell that had filled the tree house before the mushrooms appeared. Her body tingled with energy, and goose flesh rose on her skin. She felt like running and laughing and crying and screaming, all at the same time.

She opened her eyes, expecting something extraordinary—she didn't quite know what—but the tree house was more or less the same as it was before. Everything was in perfect order. There was no sign of the faerie or the redcaps.

But it had been real—hadn't it? Her heart sank. If it had been, there would be some sign of the faeries, aside from the palm-sized locket that lay cold against her chest.

Such a strange dream, though. Her sister would say it was from getting so upset. Vira was always saying things like that—things that made everything Jade's fault. Maybe her sister was right. If Jade went home now, her mother might be there to offer her warm milk with honey and to stroke her hair. That sounded really good about now.

She climbed down the tree and dropped to the ground. The trees around her gleamed in the afternoon sun like silver, and leaves bright and glittery as gold shone in the canopy above and littered the ground below. Everything, from the silver trunks to the golden roses, was covered in frost, and icicles dripped from some of the overhanging branches, catching the light like prisms. The scent of apples was stronger outside, where it mixed with the smell of snow, and she could hear the tinkling of bells on the breeze.

Kneeling, she picked up one of the frost-encrusted leaves and rubbed it between her fingers. It was cold, slick as real metal, and with pressure became a fine gold powder that coated her skin. She wasn't in Oakspring anymore, that was for sure. Was she dreaming? She pinched herself, but all she managed to do was hurt herself.

Laughter—a friendly sound, unlike the elves—came from somewhere above her. She looked up to see the faerie perched on an icy twig in one of the strange silver trees, swinging its legs.

"You *wish* your dreams were this brilliant," the faerie said, as though it could read her mind. "Quick thinking back, there by the way! We might not have gotten away if not for you."

"Thanks!" Jade said absently, marveling at the wintry forest around her. "And good hunch."

"The Sun King didn't tell me what to do after I gave you the locket," the faerie said, "but I figured he wouldn't leave us without a way out."

"What is this place?" Jade asked. Had it always been possible to get here through the tree house? And if so, why hadn't she been here before? It was like an answer to her dreams.

"You're in the Feywild," the pixie said, leaping off the twig and taking flight. "My home—home to the faeries, and the Forever Court of the fabulous Sun King." She swooped in a graceful circle around the icy tree house. "Isn't it wonderful?"

"It's beautiful," Jade said honestly. It looked just like Golden Leaf, the place from her sister's stories—down to the metallic gold leaves. It was as if she had been transported into a faerie tale—and in a very real way, she supposed she had been. She and the pixie grinned at each other. Then her grin faded as she remembered something she'd read in *A Practical Guide to Faeries*. "But this can't be the Feywild. When you enter the Feywild, you appear at the Pool of Keys."

"That true," the pixie said, "If you're a boring, normal person. But you're with me—a pixie! And we have our own paths." The little pixie looked very pleased with herself.

"I'm Pip," the faerie said, before Jade could answer. She held out her tiny hand, which Jade shook with her little finger. "I was sent by the Sun King himself on a super-secret, super-important mission to give you the locket and bring you back to the Forever Court."

"Pleased to meet you. I'm . . ." Jade paused.

Pip had called her Vira Wyvernsting before. Jade wondered if this was a bad time to mention her name. The pixie might be upset and take her back home to Oakspring. Worse, she'd probably make Jade show her where her sister was so Vira could once again have all the fun.

"You're Vira Wyvernsting. I know!" Pip laughed. "We've been listening to your stories for ages. You're a hard girl to track down. But I did it—all by myself, against all odds!—and now I get to bring you back to the Forever Court so you can fight the Ice Queen and end the war."

Jade forced a smile and nodded, though she had no real idea what Pip was talking about other than mistaking her for her sister.

"Speaking of which, we'd better get moving." Pip's dragonfly wings brushed Jade's cheek and she felt a thrill. There was a faerie on her shoulder!

"Feel that chill?" Pip asked.

Jade shivered. A light, powdery snow had begun to fall, and the frost coating on the trees grew thick and white. She began to wish she'd brought a cloak, but there had been no need back in Oakspring, where it was autumn. Where she wasn't anymore, because she was in the real Golden Leaf. Having an adventure.

"That means winter faeries are nearby. Redcaps or winter elves. It won't be long before the Ice Queen's minions, the redcaps, find their way back into the Feywild, and we do not want to be here when they come through," Pip said. "Boy, are they going to be mad! I mean, you think I get in trouble when I fail the Sun King—I hear the Ice Queen encases them in ice when they fail her."

"That's awful!" Jade said.

"Yes, but they're awful." Pip shrugged. "Besides, they're the ones dumb enough to go back to the queen and tell her they've failed. It's not like she could do anything to them if they never went back to her." Pip paused thoughtfully. "Maybe she freezes them because she gets lonely. Can an evil person get lonely?"

"Anyone can get lonely," Jade said, thinking back to when her sister had abandoned her for her new, stuck-up friends. If not for Pip, Jade's birthday would have been the loneliest day of the year. "Maybe that's why the redcaps return to the Ice Queen too."

Pip laughed. "No, redcaps are just dumb. The queen told them their toes would fall off if they didn't report back to her, and they believe her." Jade fought to control a grin. Pip put her hands on her hips. "I'm not kidding! Redcaps really are that dumb!"

"How dumb are they?" Jade asked. *That* sounded like the beginning of a joke.

"Redcaps," Pip began theatrically, "are so dumb, they think that if they cross a river, their souls will be eaten by the water faeries." Pip started giggling.

Jade smiled uneasily. Could water faeries really do that? And could they do it to people aside from redcaps?

"Redcaps are so dumb, they wear iron boots, even though it pains them, because they're afraid if they don't the earth faeries will gobble them up from below." Pip laughed so loud, it echoed off the trees.

Jade stared at Pip in horror. She couldn't imagine what was funny about being eaten, and that laughter was sure to attract unwanted attention!

Pip wiped a tear away with the back of her hand. "Redcaps"—and Jade caught a glimpse of something out of the corner of her eye—"are so dumb . . ."

She focused on the tree house behind them, squinting to make out the details. Nothing. Pip hiccupped amid her laughter. Jade breathed a sigh of relief and kept walking. The stories were starting to get to her!

". . . they believe that if their red caps ever dry out, they'll die!"

Jade caught a flash of red and the glint of steel.

"Pip!" Jade gasped, the color draining from her face.

"They really do, I swear. And stories say"—Pip lowered

her voice to a spooky whisper—"they keep their caps red with the blood of their victims!"

"Redcaps!" Jade shouted, pointing back at the tree house just as redcaps came boiling out the window and trapdoor.

The horrible little old men fixated on Jade immediately—or rather, on something on her chest. Jade put a hand down to the locket but quickly drew her hand away—it burned her skin, it was so cold. And worse, it glittered so brightly in the sunlight it might as well have been screaming, "Target!"

Pip dived off Jade's shoulder.

"Fly for it!" Pip said. "Follow me!" She zipped off through the trees and was quickly lost in the silver trunks and golden canopy.

Gritting her teeth, Jade tucked the icy metal locket under her shirt, so that it would no longer catch the sun. Then she sprinted after Pip.

In moments, the ground was blanketed in snow. It was as if the arrival of the redcaps had turned the flurries into a full-fledged winter storm. Gusts of wind carrying tiny snowflakes buffeted her, and it was impossible to make out the tiny faerie against the white and silver snowscape. There were no footprints from the pixie, but the snow was collecting heavily enough on the ground that Jade fancied even if the pixie had run on the ground, her footprints would have been filled up by the time she came across them.

"Pip, where are you?" Jade shouted, struggling to keep up her pace through the snow. She looked back over her shoulder. The redcaps were gaining on her, just like before, steam coming from mouths filled with needle-sharp teeth. Only this time, there would be no tree house escape. "Pip! I can't outrun them."

But Pip was nowhere in sight. Jade was on her own. She ran as fast as she could, hoping to get a lead early on before she got tired. Maybe she could lose them in the snow. But the drumming of the redcap's iron boots behind her let her know she would never get enough distance for that to work. She had to think of something, and fast, or risk becoming the latest batch of dye for the redcaps' hats. Her mind worked furiously. What would Vira Wyvernsting do? No. What would *Jade Farstar* do . . .

Jade Farstar was brave and clever. She would face the redcaps down, fearlessly, with some ingenious trick that left the *redcaps* running away from *her*. What had Pip said about the redcaps? That they were really dumb, more than dumb. They were gullible.

Redcaps are so dumb, they think that if they cross a river, their souls will be eaten by the water faeries.

Just then Jade saw the glint of water, almost iced over, in the distance. Yes!

A redcap's claws brushed her leg. The locket grew so cold against her chest she gasped and her teeth chattered.

She put on an extra burst of speed. How helpful! The locket grew cold the closer the winter faeries got to her. If only she could tell the locket when to stop, before it froze her lungs solid!

The river came into view, a wide river the color of liquid diamonds, whose waters were choked with bits of ice. The water looked cold enough to freeze her to the marrow if she fell in. Without stopping to think whether it was a good idea or not, she leaped onto the nearest disk of ice and spun around, gritting her teeth against the cold as water splashed up on her calves.

"Stop!" she commanded, and she squeezed her eyes shut, expecting to be bowled over, dumped in the icy water, or sliced in two by a redcap's wicked iron scythe at any moment. Please let Pip's stories be true, she thought. Please let Pip's stories be true . . .

Jade heard a fantastic crashing, but nothing hit her.

When she opened her eyes, the redcaps stood or lay scattered all along the border to the river, some rubbing their heads, all doing their best to keep from touching the water.

"I am the water faerie of this river," Jade said, using her best spooky voice.

The redcaps looked at each other and scratched under their dripping red caps with their claws.

Jade tried not to think about what made those caps red. "I command you to leave without putting so much as a toe in my waters, or else"—she bared her teeth and growled—"I'll eat your souls!" Holding her pose, she tried to seem as fierce and fearless as a proper water faerie should. But her heart beat wildly in her chest.

To her surprise, the redcaps all turned and ran back the way they'd come, stumbling over each other in their attempts to get away from her. And the farther away the redcaps got, the warmer the amulet—and the air around her—grew.

She gave a quick look around to make sure the redcaps were running from her, not some actual water faerie, and then she hopped to the next block of ice, making her way across the river.

Just then, Pip came flying back at top speed through the trees, clutching something red in her hands and wearing a tiny skullcap of the same color over her own pink and green hair.

"That was *amazing*," Pip said, flying up to her. "Really clever. I didn't know you could do that!"

"Neither did I," Jade said.

"Sorry I didn't get here sooner," Pip said. "I flew as fast as I could."

"It's all right," Jade said. And to her surprise, it was. She had escaped the redcaps all on her own.

"Here, put this on before they figure out your trick and come back." Pip handed her the red thing, which turned out to be a red hat. "That's what I went to go get. Now the redcaps won't attack us. Redcaps are so dumb, they're afraid that if they kill one of their own, they'll be cursed forever. So even though we don't look like redcaps, they won't risk it if we wear a red cap."

Jade removed her paper crown, which had somehow managed to stay on despite the two flights from the redcaps and the journey to the Feywild, gave it one last look, and tossed it to the ground. She wouldn't be needing *that* anymore. Pip gasped.

"Oh no!" Pip cried. "You don't have black hair!" Jade's hands shot up to her hair, which was blonde as a dandelion. No, she didn't have black hair. Vira had black hair.

"Wait, it's not what you think," Jade said. Now she'd messed up. She'd let the faerie believe she was Vira, just for a few minutes of adventure, and now Pip was angry with her. The pixie would probably not even lead her home, but leave her stranded in the middle of the forest with the redcaps while she went to find the good sister. Selfish, selfish, selfish. How was she going to get herself out of this one?

"You're not Vira Wyvernsting at all, are you?" Pip said.

"I didn't mean to . . ." Jade started, but how could she not mean to? She hadn't told Pip she was Vira Wyvernsting, but she hadn't said she wasn't either, and that was just as bad.

"This can't be happening," Pip said. "The Sun King will have my wings when he finds out."

"I wanted to tell you, I really did!" Jade said. "But I . . ."

"Please don't tell the Sun King," Pip begged.

". . . didn't want you to take me back home." Jade continued. "They're all ignoring me there, or treat me like I'm a baby or something, and it's my birthday and I just wanted—" Suddenly the impact of what Pip said hit Jade. "Wait, you're not going to make me go back home?"

"It wasn't supposed to be you—it was supposed to be Vira Wyvernsting," Pip said. "And the locket, once you put it on, it doesn't come off."

"What do you mean it doesn't come off?" Jade cried, her hands flying to the chain.

"Please?" Pip said. The pixie looked like she was about to cry. Her wings trembled along with her lower lip. "I would get in so much trouble."

"All right," Jade agreed, swallowing the lump in her throat and lowering her hands. She would deal with that particular problem later. The faerie had to be exaggerating. She could probably break the chain with her bare hands.

"Oh thank you, thank you, thank you!" Pip flew up and hugged Jade around the neck. Then the faerie pulled the red cap over Jade's head and tucked her blonde hair under it. "It'll be our secret. Right . . . Vira Wyvernsting?"

Jade made a face. "Right." *That* was going to take some getting used to, but there were worse things one could be called. It was kind of like being a masked hero—mysterious, secretive. It was like something Jade Farstar would do.

Jade grinned. "Now, which way out of here?"

Chapter Four

The snow was falling thick now, and Jade's toes were starting to go numb. She stamped her feet, hoping to get some feeling back into them, to no avail. They'd been walking through the ice-encased forest for what seemed like forever. At first it had been gorgeous, but over time, cold, hunger, and exhaustion sapped her excitement.

Faeries smaller than Pip drifted around like fireflies. Their bodies each glowed a different color of the rainbow, lighting up the forest like a holiday festival.

One landed delicately on Jade's nose and stood on tiptoe. It smelled like cinnamon and mint. She held her breath and looked back at the creature staring at her with wide, vacant eyes. It put both its tiny, cold hands on her nose for a moment, then it leaped off her nose, circled her once, and fluttered off. She released her breath.

"Did you see that?" Jade said, watching the faerie still circling above her head. "I think it likes me!"

"If shimmerlings can be said to like anything." Pip snorted, nibbling on a honeysuckle tart about the size of an apple seed. "They're kind of boring. Pretty, but vapid."

Jade remembered shimmerlings from *A Practical Guide to Faeries*. They were mostly mindless when alone, but with an almost hypnotic beauty, and they could be quite smart in swarms. More shimmerlings gathered around the one that had landed on her nose, following her.

"Well, I like them," Jade said.

"You *would* like them," Pip said, turning away and picking up her pace.

"What's that supposed to mean?" Jade asked. Her half-frozen legs protested as she worked to keep up with Pip. First her sister, then Pip. Even in the faerie world people called her stupid. What if she really was dumb? Would she even know it?

"You're the stupid one," Jade said. "Picking the wrong sister when I'm obviously so much uglier and stupider than pretty, perfect Vira Wyvernsting."

"You promised you wouldn't bring that up!" Pip said, turning on her. "Grandmom was right. You humans are distracted by every sparkly thing you see. No loyalty at all."

"That's not true," Jade said. "Shimmerlings might not be news to you, but we don't have them in our world. They're fascinating."

"I saw you first. That's all I'm saying," Pip said, sounding miserable. The pixie's ears drooped, and guilt gnawed at Jade. Was Pip actually jealous? Of her and the shimmerling? She knew what it was like to be discarded in favor of newer, shinier friends.

"You did," Jade said firmly. "And you'll always be my favorite."

"Really?" Pip said, turning around, her ears perking up. The hope in her eyes was heartbreaking.

"Promise," Jade said. The faerie flew up and hugged her around the head. Jade smiled and went cross-eyed looking at Pip as the cloud of shimmerlings swept past them in a vibrant stream of color.

When Pip pulled back, Jade could see that the shimmerlings had all gathered on an icy sculpture up ahead.

As she got closer, the shimmerlings scattered and hovered around the statue in a halo, revealing the strange sculpture to be a girl just like her, completely encased in ice. Well, not exactly like her. She noticed the girl had solid gold, almond-shaped eyes, and ears that swept into points. An elf. She reached out a hand and touched the ice over the girl's nose, but it was harder than steel and colder than the depths of winter. Clearly, it was some kind of magical ice.

"What happened to her?" Jade asked.

The girl's hair was a fiery red, and she had a gold crown of metal flames set with rubies, diamonds, and yellow topaz on her head. A matching sword, carved in the shape of leaping flame, was in a scabbard at her belt. Her shoulders were back and she had a determined cast to her eyes. One hand was over her heart. Jade's hand went up instinctively to touch the locket.

"That is why you're here," Pip said. "That is the work of the Ice Queen."

This could be me, Jade thought. But what she said was, "This is just a girl." She looked about ten, but Jade was struck by the direct, fearless look in her eyes, the way she stood with her feet planted firmly apart, and the way her hand was on her heart instead of on her sword. She looked like the kind of girl Jade would have liked to know.

"She thought she could stand up to the Ice Queen and end the war," Pip said. "But she wasn't strong enough, and the queen froze her."

"This is what the Ice Queen does to those who stand up to her?" Jade said. She thought about the parents, friends, and home this girl surely had. What do they think happened to her? "Gods." And the faeries wanted Jade to fight the Ice Queen?

Pip laughed. "Don't worry, that won't happen to you," Pip said as the shimmerlings slipped away from the statue and into the night, leaving them alone in the darkening woods. "You're much too clever!"

Doubt gnawed at Jade. Maybe she should urge Pip to get her sister. It wasn't too late. She hadn't met the Sun King yet, and they hadn't gotten all that far. And as much as she hated to admit it, this was clearly beyond her skills. This was dangerous, something her sister was far better at. Jade shivered with both cold and fear.

"Come on, Vira Wyvernsting," Pip said, pulling at Jade's hand. "We're not safe here. If we stay too long, one of the Ice Queen's spies will spot us."

Jade looked around. The icy trees suddenly seemed more threatening, particularly without the shimmerlings to lighten the place up. It was getting dark.

"More redcaps?" Jade asked.

"And worse," Pip confirmed. "We're almost to the Summerfields, and after that, it's only a short flight to the Garden of Dreams. We can sleep there for the night." Pip laughed. "We might not even have a choice about the matter."

Chapter Five

Jade tore her eyes away from the eerie statue and allowed Pip to lead her away. She noticed Pip keeping an eye on her, but couldn't really hide her uneasiness. She wasn't even the right sister. How was she supposed to save the faeries?

Before long, just as Pip said, the snow gave way, revealing a strange, oversized garden in which the blades of grass were the size of trees, and mushrooms loomed like oversized, white and purple umbrellas.

She passed a dandelion stalk as thick as her waist, and looked up just in time to see an errant breeze send its seeds flying. Each seed was about the size of her head. I hope the insects aren't similarly sized, she thought.

Pip kept her distracted with an unending stream of prattle about the Sun King and the Ice Queen, and the war they had been fighting for as long as the pixie could remember. Though the Feywild was split into two parts—the Winter Kingdom and the Summer Kingdom—the Ice Queen wanted to rule it all, but they couldn't let that happen because then the summer faeries would all die.

And then Pip went on about how the Sun King had sent Pip to find their last hope: Vira Wyvernsting. Jade winced at hearing her sister's name again—she hoped it wouldn't matter too much that she was the wrong girl.

With the locket, Vira Wyvernsting would help find a way to stop winter from encroaching, defeat the Ice Queen, and end the war, Pip continued. If Vira couldn't do it, no one could.

Jade's stomach grumbled irritably, distracting her from her worries. It occurred to her that she hadn't eaten since breakfast. Pip had offered her some of her honeysuckle tarts, but the pixie's food, however tempting it looked, was too small to do any more than tease her stomach. She thought wistfully of the full biscuit she'd left in the faerie box. As though the faeries could even carry a biscuit of that size! Why hadn't she checked the faerie box before leaving the tree house?

Just when she thought her stomach couldn't get any tighter, she smelled something that brought tears to her eyes—baked apples with plenty of cinnamon and sugar.

"Don't even think about it," Pip said, interrupting herself midstory.

Jade looked where the pixie was looking and saw a grown woman, about a head shorter than Jade, with great knobby joints and a dress that looked like it was probably her only one—and none too clean at that. She looked like someone's wizened grandmother, sitting in front of the smoldering fire outside of her filthy hut in the shade of a towering, tree-sized blade of grass. Humming to herself, she used her shoe to prod at several blackened, wrapped bundles in the ashes of the fire. The smell of apples intensified when she poked at them.

A bird as blue as the sky landed on a giant, capsized mushroom cap near the old woman and started singing. The old woman's eyes twinkled with tears, and she reached out a hand as if to smooth its feathers. Then a man's voice, half whine and half growl, yelled out, "Woman! Woman, I need you." And the old woman's head snapped up. After a moment of indecision, she waddled off into the grass forest in the direction of the voice.

Jade breathed in the scent of baked apples again—just as delectable as before. The old woman couldn't possibly deny them an apple or two when they were so hungry. Her stomach growled in agreement.

"Let's go while she's distracted," Jade said, her eyes on the apples roasting in the fire.

"What?" Pip squeaked. "No, we've got to get out of here. Do you have any idea what she would have done to that bird?"

"But I'm starving," Jade said. She would have asked, but

the old woman had wandered off, and who knew how long it would be before she got back? It wasn't really stealing. More borrowing, really. Besides, it was just apples. "What's she going to do, eat us?"

"Maybe!" Pip said. "Do you really want to find out?"

Jade didn't answer. She started sneaking forward, rolling from her heels to the balls of her feet like she saw her sister practice at home. To her excitement, it was actually effective. If only her sister could see her now.

"You know what's good? The food at the Forever Court. It's really good, so much better than baked apples," Pip said, glancing around and behind her and wrapping her arms around herself. "Come on, we can't stop now. We're not far! Besides, the Sun King will kill me if I don't get you there by morning!"

"Oh would you stop worrying?" Jade whispered. "You sound like my sister. This won't take a minute."

The baked apples were wrapped in smoldering, charred cloth. She knew *A Practical Guide to Faeries* said not to eat faerie food, but if she didn't eat something soon, she was sure she'd die of hunger, and then it wouldn't matter if she didn't like the taste of human food anymore anyway. Tearing off her red cap to use as a makeshift basket, Jade used the toe of her shoes to roll a couple of the apples out of the ashes. Besides, these smelled delicious! She plucked the first one up and dropped it immediately.

"I'm no shimmerling, scared of shadows," Pip said, "but that is no ordinary old woman."

"Well, if you're not a shimmerling, then stop acting like it," Jade said as she sucked on her burned fingertips. Where was snow when you needed it? She looked around until she found two sturdy, long sticks. "Help me get some apples if you want us to go sooner." Using the sticks, she managed to pick up two of the apples and deposit them into the red cap.

"Vira Wyvernsting!" Pip said.

"I told you," Jade said, "nothing's going to—"

And that's when she saw the old woman. She was holding something dripping and wrapped in sackcloth, but whatever it was, she dropped it the moment she saw Jade.

"Mine!" the old woman shrieked, pointing at them with a trembling, clawed finger. "Thieves!" And with that, she started to grow. Her knotty joints shook, and her limbs lengthened. Her tangled red hair grew bushy and long, and muscles blossomed on her arms and legs. She let out an unearthly howl.

Jade and Pip screamed as well and started scrambling backward. When the old woman straightened again, she was three times her previous height—and wrapped in monstrous amounts of muscle.

Spriggans, that's what they were called. She should have known! Jade had read about these creatures. Normally kid-sized, when angered, they grew into giants—and this spriggan definitely looked angry now. She'd only read about the male spriggans—this one must be one of the rare lady spriggans. Times must be rough, if she had to resort to eating apples instead of meat. Or maybe, that was what had been in the sackcloth . . .

"Run!" Jade cried at the same time as Pip said, "Fly!"

"This way," Pip said, and she shot off in the same direction they'd been moving before.

Jade rushed through the grass, making no move to silence her footsteps now. She clutched the red cap to her chest, hearing the crashing steps of the old woman behind her. The spriggan wasn't as fast as the redcaps, but she had much longer legs than Jade.

"Scoundrels! Pickpockets! Robbing an old woman!"

Pip zipped above them, drawing green balls from a seemingly bottomless sack and pelting the spriggan's head with them so that they exploded in sticky gobs of glue or bursts of smoke. But Pip's efforts only slowed the spriggan, and after each distraction faded, the spriggan seemed redder and angrier than before.

"It's too big!" Pip cried.

Jade thought furiously about what she'd learned about the spriggans, but couldn't think of any weaknesses. There were no trees she could climb, and no holes she could duck into.

She cut a corner sharply and bumped into the stem of an oversized buttercup. The flower bowed its head, dumping buckets worth of water over the trailing spriggan. The spriggan sputtered.

"Crooks!" the spriggan said. "Cruel humans and evil pixies!"

"Speak for yourself, you mean old hag!" Pip shouted back. She threw a green pellet that released a sound like a thousand people laughing right in front of the hag, making her hop backward.

Jade looked back over her shoulder to see the drenched spriggan's ungainly arms outstretched as the old woman ran headlong into a dandelion stalk, sending its melon-sized seeds flying.

Without thinking, Jade leaped and grabbed one of the seeds with one hand, still clutching the red cap in the other. The breeze whipped her up into the air with astonishing speed. If she'd been wearing her cap, she'd have surely lost it.

She was flying!

"Come back here with my apples!" the spriggan shouted. "Thieves!"

The wind tangled Jade's hair and pulled at her dress.

Looking down, she saw her toes barely touching the tips of the grass blades below. Pip flew up and zipped around her, making Jade dizzy. "That's the Garden of Dreams up ahead," Pip shouted, pointing. "If we can get there, we'll be home free!"

Jade tightened her grip on the seed. When she looked up, what she saw was magical: a glistening, snow white castle with tall spires and a gold-wrought fence stood surrounded by a sea of flowers that could only be the Garden of Dreams. She hadn't remembered that castle from the map in her book! It must be new. As she watched, red-gold lights appeared like fireflies along the walls and gates of the castle so that it glowed like sunset.

"With luck, we'll eat breakfast in the Forever Court!" Pip said.

But it seemed Jade's luck was at an end: the breeze sputtered out.

"No!" she cried. "I'm falling! Pip, help!"

"Hang on, I've got you!" Pip said, holding on to the back of Jade's dress. For a moment, it looked as though the tiny faerie would be able to hold Jade aloft. And then the fabric of Jade's dress ripped.

Jade went plummeting, and Pip shot up into the air, propelled by the sudden drop in weight.

Pip smashed into a tree branch above her.

"Pip, no!" Jade screamed.

Chapter Six

Jade squeezed her eyes shut as the forest floor rushed up to meet her, trying not to imagine what it would feel like to hit the ground. But instead of splattering on the hard ground, she bounced.

She'd landed in the spongy cap of an electric blue mushroom. She bounced again and looked up just in time to grab the tip of an oversized blade of grass.

She swung herself onto its blade, then slid on it all the way to the ground, the wind pulling at her hair and a grin tugging at her lips. She landed with a plop in a bed of normal-sized pansies.

That was actually rather fun. If she weren't running for her life, she would definitely ride that slide again!

"There's no flying away now, sweetling," the spriggan said from somewhere in the forest of grass.

Jade spotted Pip's tiny form, lying unconscious not five feet away in a bed of wildflowers.

The spriggan seemed not to notice. "Be a good human

and tell me where you are, and I'll just nibble the tips of your fingers for the trouble you've caused me."

Jade got to her feet as quietly as she could. Spread out before her was a garden—a normal-sized garden—thick with the scents of jasmine and rose. The roses, yellow as the sun in the center and pumpkin orange on the tips, climbed a trellis of woven white branches over a garden of wildflowers.

Curiously, one of the roses lifted off the stem it sat upon—revealing that it was actually the hair of a small pixie-like creature. It blinked at her sleepily. Oh no. The spriggan would surely eat this quiet, snacklike creature. Jade held a finger to her lips, but to her distress, the rose-faerie shook its head, sprinkling yellow pollen everywhere, sat up, and yawned. Loudly.

Grass blades rustled and the spriggan's voice became louder and clearer. Jade could almost picture the spriggan descending upon her.

"Ah, thought you could get away, did you?" the spriggan said. "Thought you could run and hide after stealing my food."

The creature flew up on wings that resembled giant rose petals and settled on Jade's finger. The smell of roses was almost overpowering. "Seriously!" Jade whispered. "You have to—" The rose-creature began to sing a soft, wordless lullaby.

The smell of the roses and the soothing tones of the lullaby were intoxicating. Breathing in deeply, Jade became aware of subtleties in the scent—rose with underlying jasmine, cinnamon, and strawberries. She closed her eyes and took another long sniff of the heady perfume. The lullaby swelled, filling her mind with dreams of flying, riding griffons, and proving her sister wrong.

Then she realized what was happening. These were petals—they were putting her to sleep. The petal on her finger smiled at her and continued to sing, pollen swirling from its petal tresses.

"No! I can't! I—" Jade yawned again. Her limbs felt as if they were stuffed with hot sand.

"Don't bother running now," the spriggan said.

Jade didn't want to run. Running was so much work. She just wanted to lie down and go to sleep. It had been a long day—her birthday—and all she wanted was a good nap. Was that too much to ask? For her birthday? There was some reason she couldn't though. Wasn't she just saying, "I can't"?

"I know you're around here somewhere . . ." the spriggan said. "It's only a matter of time before I find you." The spriggan's voice went through her like lightning. She had to get out of there before the petals' magic made her easy prey.

Forcing her limbs into action, Jade half ran, half fell, so slowly she could have been running through molasses, scooping up unconscious Pip with one hand. As she passed the trellis, the wildflowers in the garden all nodded in an invisible breeze and then fluttered into the air, revealing themselves to be petals as well, swarming around her like flowers caught in a windstorm, all singing with one, ethereal voice, and trailing heady clouds of perfume and waxy, yellow pollen.

That was it! It was the singing. She had to cover her ears, if she were ever to escape the petals' song. The cap with the offending red apples was still clutched in one hand, wet and warm with the drippings from the baked fruit. Pip was in the other.

She was so hungry! But her ears ached, and she had no more time. Dumping the apples on the ground, and putting Pip in a pocket, she pressed her hands to her ears, blocking out the dulcet tones of the petals' song.

The effect was immediate. With each moment, the urge to curl up and go to sleep faded, and the need to get away from the angry spriggan rose.

She turned, still holding her ears.

"I'm so sorry," she whispered to the pixie. "This is all my fault."

Then she thought of an idea. Maybe the spriggan hadn't noticed the petals, or better yet, maybe she had, but didn't know about the petals' sleep-inducing song. It was a long shot, but it was possible that the spriggan had never wandered so far from her domain. And besides, it might be Jade's only chance at getting the spriggan off their trail. She needed to stop running sometime.

Raising her head and her voice before she could second-guess herself, she called out to the spriggan. "Come and get me, then!"

The spriggan's eyes lit up. "Ah, there you are, thief," she said. She took one step forward into the trellis and was immediately engulfed in petals, song, and perfume. It was beautiful, like a storm of flowers. After two more steps into the garden, the spriggan yawned loudly and fell over with a crash, sending petals and flowers and leaves everywhere.

Jade froze a moment. Was it a trick?

The spriggan started snoring, loudly enough to be heard through the hands over her ears.

Jade let out a sigh and then quickly pressed her fingers harder over her ears. The spriggan shuddered a moment, and then shrank back to her normal size. Curled up in the flowers, snoring like a baby, she looked as kind and sweet as a grandmother again. Then the petals descended on the old woman in such numbers that Jade could no longer make out her form.

What are they doing? Jade thought in horror. Are they eating her?

Jade tiptoed closer, to do what she wasn't sure. Scare

the petals away? But just then, the petals began drifting away one by one.

Jade grimaced, half expecting to see a skeleton under the blanket of flowers, but the spriggan was still all in one piece, curled up on the ground, her head lying on her hands. Her hair was all combed out and strung with daisies, and she now wore a dress woven from lilies, violets, and silk. A gentle smile was on her face, as though she were having a really good dream.

Jade looked at the apples, still wrapped, still on the ground by the spriggan. They smelled delicious. It wouldn't do to let them go to waste, not while they were still hot, and not after all that effort. Using her feet, Jade gently guided the apples along in front of her down the garden path, away from the petals and the spriggan.

Jade walked awkwardly through sunset—juggling the apples and Pip, and keeping her hands pinned over her ears—until night fell and the stars came out. Fireflies drifted through the flowers, lighting them in shades of orange and red, and the trunks of the weeping willows in the garden glowed with green moss.

Eventually, she reached an open garden with a black reflecting pool in the center. It was filled with bright gold fish each the size of her head, and was surrounded by violets, white coral bells, and buttercups.

She kicked an acorn into the bed of flowers. She watched carefully, but no heads raised from the flowers, and none looked like they were actually faeries in disguise. Then she removed her hands from her ears and took a deep breath, and was met by a pleasant aroma of flowers, but not the heady perfume of the petals. She dumped the apples out of their cap and settled the hat back on her head, not caring a bit about the sticky apple juices or the grass stains, and tucked her hair up underneath it again.

Jade plucked Pip from her pocket and laid her down on a soft bed of moss. Then she opened up the first of the apples. Bruised, but bursting with flavor, the apple was everything she had hoped for. She closed her eyes. It was the best thing she'd ever eaten. It was totally worth never wanting human food again. She would just always eat faerie food. It was so much better, anyway. Her stomach gurgled in agreement.

Then she opened her eyes and looked down at the mushy apple. It was also the only birthday cake she would be getting this year. She wondered if her family had noticed she was missing yet—if they even missed her at all.

"Mmm . . . something smells delicious," murmured Pip, stirring on her bed of moss.

"Welcome back!" Jade smiled and unwrapped the second apple. Then she swallowed, guilt sticking in her throat. "I'm so sorry I—"

"Mmmmm! Apples!" Pip said, fully awake now. She dived into the second apple, chewing her way straight through the middle with astonishing speed. "These apples were totally worth it." Pip said from inside her own apple tunnel.

"Yeah, I . . ." Jade began before she realized what Pip had said. "Wait, they were?"

"I knew you could handle the spriggan," Pip said between mouthfuls.

Jade started. She did? How did Pip know that? Jade hadn't even been sure she could handle it herself, and Pip had seemed certain they were both going to end up as spriggan snacks. Pip displayed an astonishing ability to revise history. "How'd you do that anyway?"

"The petals got the spriggan," Jade said. "I just led the spriggan to the petals."

"Petals, huh?" Pip said through mouthfuls of hot, mushy apple. "Yeah, they're easy to underestimate."

Exhaustion from the day's events finally setting in, Jade turned her attention back to her apple, listening to Pip's tales of previous adventures with petals and spriggans. Pip seemed to have a hundred tales of all the creatures in the Feywild, and personal death-defying adventures with at least half of them. While Jade wasn't sure how much she believed of the pixie's stories, it was oddly comforting to know the pixie was so unfazed.

Jade lay down, licking the apple off her fingers. The soft, velvety flowers were warm against her skin, and the stars sparkled in the black sky above. They were gorgeous in a way Jade couldn't remember ever having seen before. They reminded her of the shimmerlings and of the girl stuck in the ice. The girl who would never get home—who would never have another birthday.

"What was her name?" Jade asked.

"Who, the spriggan?" Pip asked, wrinkling her nose. "I don't know. Something awful. Like Dorkia Dumbbutt. Or Smelly Dungbottom."

"No, not her," Jade said. "The girl in the ice."

"Oh, her," said Pip. "Her name is Phoenix."

"Phoenix." Her family didn't know where she'd gone, and she was frozen in ice forever. Jade wondered how the girl had left her family, whether she had left on good terms or bad. Had she regretted anything, like fighting with her sister and storming off? Or did she, too, doubt whether she was strong enough to help the faeries? Whether there was something she would have done differently?

Too late to worry about that now. Jade was far from home, and there was no going back. She glanced over at Pip, who was sprawled in an overgrown blue rose, snoring quietly. Besides, she wasn't sure she wanted to return home. Sure it was frightening, but she had yearned her whole life for something like this. This was magical. There was a faerie sleeping beside her, she was in the land of the faeries, and the Sun King needed her to help fight the Ice Queen.

You didn't get a chance like that every day growing up in Oakspring.

But as she drifted off to sleep, the image of the girl encased in ice haunted her dreams.

Chapter Seven

They managed to reach the Forever Court before noon, which Pip claimed was early enough that she need not fear the Sun King's vengeance.

"He expects me to be a little late," Pip had confided. "After all, I'm just a pixie."

When Jade saw the golden gates of the Forever Court, with white and gold lilies and moonflowers winding between the bars, she was instantly entranced. She had been so busy looking at all the strange and beautiful things around her—faeries who fought with swords made out of thorns, faeries with insect legs, faeries with skin made of bark and a shower of leaves for hair—that she barely noticed as a satyr and a brownie shuttled her off up countless flights of stairs into a private chamber.

She had noticed once the brownie had started fitting her for dresses, however, and the satyr tried teaching her courtly etiquette.

"Put this on . . . no that!" the brownie said as it tried to find her an appropriate gown. "Why are you so tall? Can't you shrink a little for me?"

"You have such round, human feet!" The satyr stared at her. "Now, when you meet the king, flutter your fingers like flowers and courtesy! No, not like frogs, like flowers! Do my fingers look like frogs to you?"

Frankly, the satyr's fingers didn't looked like much of anything. But he was wiggling them so *insistently*. This was the kind of thing her sister was good at. Making a good first impression, handling guests, being polite . . . these were not exactly Jade's specialties.

After what seemed like hours, the brownie and the satyr pronounced her as ready as she'd ever be and left her to herself.

"Remember," Pip whispered, hovering by her ear. "Your name is Vira Wyvernsting."

"I know," Jade said

"And your hair stays under your cap," Pip said.

"I know," Jade said. No wonder they had wanted her sister. All the same, she was a little annoyed at Pip's lack of confidence in her. *Someone* had to believe in her.

"And try to act cooler than you are," Pip said, rubbing her hands together nervously.

"I know already," Jade said. Of course she remembered; she wasn't a baby. She just didn't particularly like being reminded that this whole adventure was a mistake, that she was supposed to be her sister. "I'm my snobby older sister. Can't you tell?" She lifted her chin in the air, threw back her shoulders, and pursed her lips.

"I knew I could count on you." Pip grinned. "Vira Wyvernsting."

Jade nodded. Was it just her, or did Pip look taller this morning? After the huge mushrooms and oversized blades of grass, her reference points were all messed up.

"To tell you the truth, I wanted you from the beginning," the pixie confided. "You look like a lot more fun. But the Sun King said that you were too immature, and that your older sister would be a better fit for the prophecy. Frankly, I think she's more stuffy than mature. But no one listens to me, I'm just a pixie."

"I'm not listening," Jade said. So the Sun King thought she was immature before even meeting her. They were off to a great start. This wasn't going to be awkward at all. Maybe her older sister should have come.

"See? That's what I'm talking about!" Pip said. "You're so funny! Your sister never would have answered like that. She would have tried to logically explain . . ."

Jade tuned Pip out and fidgeted with the hem of her new dress.

Woven from red and gold leaves, dusted with tiny bells that tinkled, and flared out at the bottom like an explosion of autumn, it was the simplest of the dresses she had been forced into. The brownie dressmaker thought it was much too plain and an insult to his skill, but Jade had put her foot down.

"I'm not sure I'm ready for this." Jade groaned. "I think I'm going to be sick."

"No you aren't, Vira Wyvernsting," Pip said bracingly. "You're going to be brilliant, Vira Wyvernsting!"

"I get it already!" Jade snapped. "You can stop adding that name to the end of every sentence."

"Vira Wyvernsting?" The voice came from the other side of the oak door of her preparation chamber. "The Sun King is ready for you."

"Ready," Jade whispered to herself, and then she opened the door to find the satyr dressed in a white and gold brocade jacket that shimmered as if it were made of burning feathers.

"Just one more thing," the satyr said. On closer inspection, its jacket *was* made of burning feathers. She shook her head. Faerie fashions would take some getting used to. "We need to remove that ratty old hat you have. It's just not proper to wear a hat in front of the Sun King in the Forever Court. And what is that on it anyway? Applesauce?"

"No! Don't take it off!" Jade said, holding the hat to her head as she tried to think of an excuse. "It's very important because . . . because . . ."

70

"Her head is deformed!" Pip cried. "Covered in evil sores that ooze pus. It's awful, I know. I almost died when I saw it. A curse, if I ever saw one."

"Very well," the satyr said, his nose wrinkled in disgust. "I suppose covering your head is the better part of . . . courtesy, then. If you would follow me."

The stairs that led down into the court were wide and appeared to be woven from white branches on which jasmine plants had been encouraged to grow. From the top, she could see the entire Forever Court spread below her, and it was breathtaking.

Round tables were scattered around the edges of the room, satyrs and elves and all manner of faeries dressed in their faerie best danced across a floor of hammered gold, and pixies carrying lanterns flew around.

On the right was a spread of food fit to make a king swoon, and on the left side of the room a group of satyrs played fiddles, pan flutes, and a tremendous assortment of drums. The music had the unearthly quality of dreams and seemed to vibrate her bones and set her feet to tapping. It was all she could do not to burst into dance right there. Luckily, her pressing need to not look like a fool in front of all the faeries of the Forever Court helped her clamp down on the urge. There must be some magic in that music, she thought.

On a raised dais at the far end of the room was a set

of four thrones made of branches intertwined to look like sunbursts. Two of them were filled. The larger figure, a male elf who could only be the Sun King, was dressed elegantly in white robes embroidered in gold, while the other, the Sun Prince, Jade assumed, was dressed similarly in slacks and a tunic of an enviably simple but elegant design. Both wore delicate crowns that matched their thrones, and had pointed ears that peeked out from behind their hair, but while the king's hair was sun blond, the prince's was so pale as to be almost white. Just as her eyes settled on the Sun King, his eyes—solid gold—alit on hers.

"Vira Wyvernsting!" A hush went over the room when the Sun King stood, and all the eyes in the room turned to her. She could feel her face flush as red as her dress as "Vira Wyvernsting" was repeated through the crowd along with whispers of "the prophecy."

"Welcome to the Forever Court," the Sun King said as he descended the stairs from his dais to the center of the room. The faeries all bowed and parted before him like blades of grass nodding in the breeze. The satyr gave her a push from behind, and she stumbled down the first few stairs before catching herself and walking to the king in her best imitation of demure.

Behind him, the Sun Prince stayed seated. Jade's eyes narrowed. So, this was the boy who thought she wasn't as good as her sister, was he? He didn't look like much. In fact, he looked boring. He had a strange half smile on his lips. What was that about? Did he think something was funny?

"You've got this, Vira Wyvernsting!" Pip whispered, drawing Jade's attention back to the Sun King.

"Just don't leave me," Jade whispered back.

"You have come just in time," the Sun King said, grasping her hands in his. She was startled by how smooth his hands were—like glass. He turned to the watching faeries and raised his voice. "The human girl has come wearing the locket, just as was prophesied! Her name is Vira Wyvernsting, and on the third night from the day she entered the Feywild, according to the prophecy, she will lead us to victory against the Ice Queen." The gathered faeries erupted in cheering and clapping.

Jade smiled nervously. What exactly did he mean by "lead"? But to avoid making a fool of herself in public, she pretended she knew and waved to the assembled faeries. They loved that, yelling even louder.

The king smiled at her and nodded at the summer faeries—the pixies, satyrs, sun elves, and other faeries of the summer court. Then he lowered his voice. He sounded warm, but far less confident than he had been when he addressed his people. "Enjoy the party. It's in your honor, and I'm sure you'll have precious little time for fun in the next few days."

Jade looked into the shining, hopeful faces of all the summer faeries and struggled to hold onto her smile. They were all waiting for her to save them. Was that why Vira had been practicing with elves? Had Vira secretly been preparing to save the faeries? All the elves, the archery, the relentless training—and why the faeries had wanted Vira instead of Jade suddenly made sense.

"We are all counting on you, Vira Wyvernsting," the Sun King said. But she wasn't Vira. What would they do to her if they found out she wasn't the right girl—that she didn't know what to do?

"Someone has stolen my trove, which contains all my magic," the Sun King continued, "and without it, I cannot defend my court. You are our only hope. If you cannot find the trove to save us, all of this splendor—and all the pixies, shimmerlings, satyrs, petals, and other summer faeries—will disappear, encased in ice, buried in snow, and frozen in a cold that never ends."

"Like Phoenix," Jade said.

"Yes," the Sun King said, getting a far off-look in his eyes. "Like Phoenix."

Jade's mind was reeling. She had thought that the king would tell her what to do. But the Sun King seemed to think she knew what to do, that she would lead them! Vira would have known what to do.

An awful mistake had been made. Somehow, she had to

figure out what she was supposed to do to save the faeries without letting them discover she was the wrong girl. And without getting killed. Or imprisoned in ice. Or . . .

"As I said, you don't have much time," the Sun King said. "The Ice Queen's ice is already encroaching on my kingdom's lands. If you need anything from me, seek out Aron," the king said, gesturing at a pale faerie without a mouth. "He is my right hand, and he will be able to help you." The Sun King turned and started to walk away. "Now, do whatever it is you must do. Save my people."

"But your majesty!" Jade cried after him. "I don't—" The faeries in the court watched her expectantly, waiting to hear whatever she was going to say, waiting for her to let them know how she was going to save them. "I don't know what to do," she whispered.

Then the Sun King was out of sight, and the faeries closed in. Jade tried to follow, but she couldn't manage to push through the crowd.

With a sigh, she turned to the faeries so eager to introduce themselves.

"I'm so glad to meet you, Vira Wyvernsting!" said a tall, lithe elf with red eyes and hair as white as snow.

"Vira Wyvernsting, try some of these!" said a passing satyr, who had golden fur and black, curling horns on his head. "Sunny apples, the Forever Court specialty!"

"Do you like my dress?" a brownie with bright blue eyes said, twirling in place. "It's a living dress, made of mice!"

"You must dance with me, Vira Wyvernsting," begged a green-haired thorn, its skin green as grass and its hair spiky as its namesake. "Just one dance!"

Vira Wyvernsting, Vira Wyvernsting, Vira Wyvernsting! Before long Jade had shaken hands with every faerie at least once—some two or three times—and tasted everything the kitchens had to offer, and whirled across the floor in a dozen or so "last dances" with this satyr and that elf.

Every time she whirled across the floor, she was terrified of some of her hair coming loose, of being discovered. Whenever she was introduced to someone, she was certain she was going to slip up and tell them her real name, or not answer to her sister's name. She was certain that she must look suspicious. It was only a matter of time before someone put the pieces together, and then they would be so angry with her. And on top of that, none of them seemed to know anything more than she did about how she was supposed to save them.

She was thirsty, tired, and feeling very out of her depth.

How could she save the faeries when she couldn't even get her own sister to tell her a story on her birthday? When the elves back home thought she was a baby? She should have made Pip go back and get her sister while they still had a chance, before Jade had been introduced to the court as the savior of the faeries.

It was all too much. She was sweating profusely and she felt dizzy.

She caught sight of the delicious-looking punch in the decadent, faun-shaped fountain on the right side of the room, and suddenly it was all she wanted. The punch was a light gold, with embers swimming within it like fish. Water beaded on the outside of the fountain, as though the drink were still cold. It looked like the most refreshing beverage in the world.

She scooped up some punch in one of the seashell-shaped cups and was just about to take a sip when she caught sight of something in the reflection of the golden liquid: two of the embers swirled into dragons, each holding a mirror in its claws. And then the dragons opened their jaws and screamed so loud the sound rang her head like a bell. She shook her head to clear the horrible ringing and looked around, but no one else seemed to have noticed. She looked back at the punch, but there was no sign of the dragons. A clue? But what did it mean?

Before she could examine it further, she had a nagging sensation between her shoulder blades. She turned to see a tall, thin, pearl-hued faerie with solid black eyes and who seemed to be missing a mouth. It was Aron, the Sun King's right hand. A banshrae, she thought to herself, one of the faeries whose mouths had been stolen by the Ice Queen.

Come with me, she heard in her head. His voice was flutelike and soft. The banshrae? He nodded. *I can help you. Come alone.* Then he turned and began making for the far side of the room.

"Wait!" she said, dropping the seashell cup. As quickly as she dared, she began pushing her way through the crowd after the banshrae, trying to keep him in sight as the twirling, dancing faeries jostled and pulled at her. She was halfway across the room when someone caught her elbow.

She turned to find herself staring at the Sun Prince.

"Vira Wyvernsting," he said. His intense, solid blue eyes searched her face and his breath smelled like cinnamon.

"I'm sorry," Jade said, looking for a way around the prince. "But I'm kind of busy."

The banshrae was already at the other side of the room and halfway to the door by the foot of the stairs. She couldn't lose him now. He was the only clue she had!

The prince smiled. It was not a nice smile. He was clearly used to getting his way. "Busy? With what?"

She bit her tongue and reminded herself that this insolent boy was important—the son of the Sun King—and that she should think before she responded.

But what could she say? That she was seeing things in the punch? That the banshrae wouldn't talk to her with him around? Or that she was afraid of being found out and not being able to help them, and really just wanted some time alone to figure her way out of it all? That would go over well.

It was too late now anyway. The banshrae had disappeared through the door at the foot of the stairs. She would have to find a way to track him down later.

She turned back to the prince and sighed. "What can I do for you?"

"So glad you could make time for me," he said, letting go of her elbow. Was that sarcasm in his voice? "Dance with me."

"Do I have a choice, Your Highness?" she answered sweetly, taking his hand.

His eyes flashed with annoyance, but he controlled it quickly. "Call me Frost."

Frost? That was a strange name for a summer faerie—especially for the prince of the Forever Court. Jade felt a wave of uncertainty as he led her out onto the floor and looked around, but no one else seemed to notice anything amiss.

The band took up a lively tune, and Frost spun her out onto the floor. Within heartbeats, she was exceedingly grateful for the dancing lessons the satyr had pressed upon her.

"How are you planning on stopping the Ice Queen?" Frost asked.

"What? I . . ." Jade began, flustered. She didn't even know where to begin. Was this it? Was this where she was going to get caught? Her face flushed a deep crimson, and her ears burned. She waited for him to call her out in front of everyone, ridicule her, dismiss her as a selfish child.

"Why do you think my father brought you here?" the prince snapped. "To have fun dancing at his stupid parties?" The prince gestured angrily at the festive faeries spinning and laughing and twirling across the dance floor. "We're fighting a war here, human. The ice is encroaching, and my father is convinced that the glaistig's prophecy means that *you* will be the one to end the war, and that you will do it in three nights."

"Wait, I thought the prophecy said I was going to defeat the Ice Queen," Jade said. That was an important distinction.

"First, you need a plan," Frost continued as though he hadn't heard her, spinning her faster and faster.

"I know," Jade said. "I was thinking–"

"You can't just go in there and fight her, you know," Frost interrupted.

"I don't want to 'just go in there,' " Jade said, irritated and starting to get dizzy again. He wasn't even listening to her!

"Better faeries than you have faced the Ice Queen and lost," Frost said. "*Faeries*–not human children."

"Like Phoenix. I know," Jade snapped. Was he deaf, or just really rude? Suddenly, they stopped spinning. She had to lean on the prince to keep her balance.

"What do you know about Phoenix?" Frost asked, pushing her away so he could look at her face. His hands tightened on hers.

"Let go!" she cried. "You're hurting me." The Sun Prince loosened his grip.

"Who told you about her?" he demanded. Jade was glad she hadn't told Frost about the banshrae. It probably would have gotten them both in trouble.

"I saw her frozen in the ice," she answered, glaring at him. "Pip told me she got that way because she stood up to the Ice Queen, which is apparently more than you ever did."

"That's it?" Frost said.

"She looked nice," Jade said, lifting her chin a little. "And *that's* it."

They glared at each other for a moment, neither one willing to give way. Then Frost lowered his eyes.

"She was nice," Frost said softly. That made Jade really curious. Who was this Phoenix who inspired such strong emotions in everyone? "And you are *nothing* like her." His hands loosened on hers, as though he were going to let her go. This time, she was the one to grip harder.

"No, I'm not," Jade said, anger flaring in her again as she remembered how Pip had told her that the prince had thought she wasn't as good as her sister. "But I'm all you've got, and you have to help me."

The Sun Prince looked at her, considering her request the way her cat, Fluffy, considered her requests to come when called.

"Very well," he said. "You're no use to anyone if you don't know anything."

"Thank you," Jade said. She'd take what she could get.

"Don't thank me," Frost said. "What I'm telling you will probably get you killed."

"Thank you anyway," Jade said. "For the vote of confidence."

"Someone stole the Sun King's trove—the source of all his magic," Frost said.

"I know, he told me," Jade said.

"At the same time, the Ice Queen's trove was also stolen," Frost said. "That's when Phoenix confronted her. The Ice Queen should have been helpless, but somehow, she used her magic to freeze Phoenix. And the war is worse than ever now. The ice is drawing closer to the summer faeries' land. The queen shouldn't be able to use her ice magic anymore."

"So you're saying that the Ice Queen's trove wasn't stolen at all," Jade said.

"No," Frost said forcefully. *"Both* troves were stolen. And yet, the magic continues."

"I *got* that part—"

"*Clearly*, you didn't," Frost snapped. Jade sucked in her breath, taken aback. "Otherwise, I wouldn't need to repeat it." The Sun Prince looked away angrily. "I told my father this was too complicated for a human. I don't know why he insisted on bringing you in when he has me."

"Oh, I don't know," Jade said under her breath. "Maybe it's because you're such a jerk."

"You have no idea what you're talking about," the prince said.

"Maybe so," Jade said, finally finding her footing. "But you're not making it any easier on me!"

Just then, the dance music changed.

"Look. We both know you don't belong here," Frost said, letting go of her hands and bowing coldly. Jade felt a sudden chill. Did he know she wasn't Vira? "If you ever want to go home again, *human*, just stay out of my way. Otherwise, you'll end up as frozen as . . . as Phoenix."

"How—" Jade began.

But Frost had already slipped away through the crowd.

If the Sun King had sent her the locket, why was his son being so unhelpful? He seemed to really resent the fact that his father asked her for help. And did he know she wasn't really Vira? And if so, who would he tell? At least he hadn't given her away yet. She ran a hand along her red cap, but all her hair seemed in place. He'd just told her to stay out of the very thing his father had asked her to help with.

Where was Pip anyway? Leaving her alone with all those faeries, not one of whom had proved remotely helpful. What was the pixie thinking? Jade scanned the crowd, but could find no sign of Pip. In fact, there was no sign of any pixies at the party at all. Were pixies not allowed to attend the Sun King's parties or something?

In the midst of the bustling party, Jade suddenly felt very alone.

Chapter Eight

Pip?" Jade whispered. Faeries in colorful dresses and dapper suits twirled around, passing partners or dancing on their own. Some pressed into corners, laughing and drinking and playing games. She pushed through the crowd. "Where are you, Pip?"

She made her way out of the room through the same side exit the banshrae had used and found herself in a long, dark, narrow corridor. Looking down the corridor, she thought about turning back. But it was good to get out for a bit where she could breathe and think. Besides, she might even run into the banshrae again.

Picking up the pace—she didn't like the look of that corridor one bit—she followed its rootlike twists and turns until she emerged outside in a small patio.

Paved with round garden stones and surrounded and shaded by moss-encrusted oak trees that seemed big enough around to crawl inside, the patio looked like the perfect place to rest for a moment. Three high tables covered in draping spidersilk cloths dotted the patio. A single candle glittered at the center of each table. The candles brought attention to how dark is was—darker than it should be for such an early hour of a night that was bereft of fireflies and lanterns.

Jade stepped into the clearing, and the trees rustled as though they noticed her and were talking amongst themselves. Peering at the twisted bark, she could almost make out faces.

She heard a *thud* behind her. The door she had come through had slammed shut. The wind?

She turned slowly, just in time to see all the candles go out. Now she was night-blind as well.

The best thing she could do was make her way back to the door and to the party. This escape was becoming far from restful.

A chill breeze that smelled of rotting fish swept out from the woods, raising gooseflesh on her skin. Backing toward the patio door slowly, she examined the darkness for signs of movement.

When she reached the door, she turned quickly and tried the handle. Locked.

"Ah, you've been with the Sun Prince," said a sly voice.

Jade spun around.

"Who are you?" she asked, her voice high as a mouse's, her back pressed up against the door.

A woman lounged against the table directly behind her—Jade could have sworn that table was empty a moment ago!—resting on her elbows and giving the girl a crooked, knowing smile. The woman's long, snow white hair glittered, wet, in loose curls all the way down to her waist, and she was dressed in a waterlogged dress that didn't quite conceal the white fur on her legs or her hooves. Her lips were red as an apple's skin. She smelled like wet goat. She tilted her head back and inhaled deeply.

"His smell lingers on you still," the woman said, exhaling.

Jade started circling, facing the woman, but moving so her back was no longer against the wall.

"What do you want?" Jade said.

"You should be careful with that one, you know. In the past, he was of a very different season." The woman strolled closer languidly, each step rustling her dress and ringing with her hooves on the stone-cobbled ground.

"What do you mean? We just talked," Jade said, backing up. Looking past the woman and up at the castle behind her, she could see the lights through the window, and the faeries dancing and cavorting. What had seemed so oppressive before suddenly seemed far more comforting. "Pip!" she called. Maybe the faeries would hear her. "Pip, help!"

"What I wonder is"—the woman ignored her cries for help—"whose son is he really? Inside?"

"Come on, Pip, come on," she whispered. "Where are you when I need you?"

She heard a pounding on the door. The handle rattled, and Jade looked at it with hope in her eyes. But it failed to open.

The woman smiled. An explosion sounded on the other side, and smoke trailed out of the keyhole and under the door.

"Were you to cut him open right now"—the woman put a dripping, clawed finger to Jade's chest, right where the locket lay—"would his heart be of fire or ice?"

"Get away from me!" Jade shrieked, batting the woman's hand aside. The woman withdrew her hand with a hiss, glaring at the girl as though she meant to punish Jade for her transgression, but then the tree above groaned, rattling its branches and deepening the shadows. The woman looked up, calculating, considering.

"When Frost has lost what he once took, and you would do what he forsook"—the woman smiled, revealing a set of needlelike teeth—"find me."

A riddle? Why had the woman given her a riddle?

Jade was just about to ask when a brass serving platter went sailing through a window, sending glass shards flying.

The woman faded into the darkness, leaving a puddle of water behind.

"Vira Wyvernsting!" Pip called.

"Pip!" Jade couldn't think of a time when she was happier to see someone. "Where were you?"

"I just went to play a quick game of stickyball. Quinn started it, throwing a stickyball at me when I'd made it very clear I had important human-escorting duties to perform. And then when I came back, you were gone." Jade looked closer at the pixie and noticed she had a daisy—which was about the size of the pixie herself—still stuck to the back of her head. "I swear I didn't mean to leave you alone in there," Pip went on. "What happened? How did you get all the way out here?"

"I just had to get away, you know?" Jade said. "There were so many faeries, and Frost, I mean the Sun Prince . . ."

"You talked to the Sun Prince?" The faerie went green with envy. "Aw, you get all the fun! What'd you talk about?"

"I don't really know. He was being strange," Jade said. "And then I came out here to get some time to myself, and the door locked, and there was this creepy lady or faerie or I don't know what she was. She just disappeared." Jade pointed to the puddle the woman had left behind.

Pip looked horrified. "You mean the glaistig? How'd *she* get to the Forever Court?"

"Is that bad?" Jade said. A glaistig! Jade wondered if that glaistig was the same who had given the king the prophecy.

"It's not good. Glaistigs are dark, dangerous faeries. They spend half their time in the water and the other half on land, drifting with whatever faction seems to be winning in whatever games they are tracking. They're traders in secrets and prophecies—for a steep price," the pixie said. "And they can't stray far from the water for long—otherwise they'll die. So it must have been important."

"Well, she said something about the Sun Prince," Jade said, thinking back. "That he was also the son of the Ice Queen."

"That's true," Pip admitted.

Why hadn't she been told that before? She supposed it hadn't come up—she'd just gotten there after all—but on the other hand, it certainly seemed relevant.

"And that she wondered where his true allegiance lay—whether we could trust him or not," Jade added, watching Pip closely. The pixie's eyebrows rose.

"Now that's good gossip," Pip said, rubbing her hands together. "We could get a lot of muffins for that little tidbit."

"Can we? Trust the Sun Prince, I mean?" Jade asked.

"You kind of have to, don't you?" Pip shrugged.

"I mean, he just didn't seem like he wanted me around . . . at all," Jade said. *We both know you don't belong here.* She frowned and struggled to shake away the hurt. Why did she care what some moody faerie prince thought?

"He said, 'If you ever want to go home again, *human*, just stay out of my way.' "

"That pimply faced pig pusher! How dare he call you human!" Pip gasped.

"But, Pip, I am huma—" Jade began.

"It's the principle of it!" Pip fumed.

"But that's not all he said," Jade said. "He also said we should start looking for the source of the Ice Queen's power."

"That's great!" Pip exclaimed. "That sounds much better. But how are we going to do that?"

"I don't know," Jade said, "but we have to figure it out." There was no way she was going to let the Sun Prince scare her away. Now it was a matter of honor. "Earlier there was a faerie—Aron—who said he'd help. And the king vouched for him. Speaking of which, the Sun Prince didn't seem to want me to speak to Aron either, even after his father recommended him."

"Now that's strange. Why would he do that?" Pip said. "Unless he was working against his father . . ."

"We can't be sure of that yet, but we have to find Aron," Jade said. "He's the only chance we have of getting some answers. I lost track of him somewhere around—"

"In the morning," Pip said, grabbing hold of Jade's sleeve and pulling her back. "The party's over, and even pixies need sleep."

Chapter Nine

The next morning, Jade woke up feeling remarkably refreshed, all the worries and cares of the night before washed away as though it were all just a strange but wonderful dream. Her skin was warm with sunlight, she tasted apples on her tongue, and the leaves she lay on were cool and springy. A breeze sighed across her . . . bare skin?

"Piiiiiip!" Jade shrieked, leaping up and quickly clutching an oak leaf around her—and did a double take. Her hands were gold tinged. She looked at the daisy she stood next to. It was still about the same size she was. Her human-sized dress from the Forever Court lay in a puddle around her, like a giant's nest. The brownie was going to be so upset with her. The only thing that still fit her was the locket, which had miraculously shrunk along with her.

The previous night, Pip had taken her to her home, and since Jade was too big to fit in the pixie's tree and the weather was warm as summer, the girl had slept outside on a bed of moss. The Sun King had offered to set up a bed for her in the Forever Court, but after her exchange with the Sun Prince, she felt safer in the pixie glen, a meandering patch of forest of hollowed, living trees in which nests of extended families of pixies lived.

Before bed, Pip had given her the full tour, shown her where they played stickyball, where they bathed, and where they ate their meals. These were the three most important things to a pixie.

A giggling sound made her swing around, only to fall and drop the leaf she was holding to cover herself. Scrambling for privacy, she almost forgot about the giggling until Pip fluttered down. Pip was human sized! Or rather, Jade thought, she herself was now pixie sized. What had happened?

"Good morning!" Pip said, still stifling giggles. "I thought you might want this." Pip held out a pixie-sized dress woven from spidersilk. It shimmered green-gold in the light and looked as though it would blend in perfectly with the forest. The pixie also held a smaller red skullcap for Jade's hair.

"You did this!" Jade said, trying to hold her leaf to her.

"Not me!" Pip said. "The locket brings out the faerie in you—and it looks like the faerie in you is a pixie. I'm so proud of you! I bet your sister would have been some kind of stuck-up elf or something."

A pixie? Just like Jade Farstar! She felt a thrill. Who said she couldn't grow up to be a pixie?

As she prepared the slip on the dress, she noticed it had four slits in the back—for wings, she realized. She pulled the dress on, wiggling the wings—*her* wings!—through the holes. She turned her head as far as she could and spun like a dog chasing its tail as she tried to catch sight of her wings. They were translucent green with gold striations. Before tucking her hair under her new red cap, she saw that her hair—which now floated around her head like so much dandelion floss—was a bright, burnished blonde with jade green streaks.

"Can I fly?" She flexed the muscles that seemed to harness the wings to her back. All four of the wings fluttered, and she caught a little air. She gasped.

"I don't know." Pip smirked. "Can you?" And with that, Pip took off. "Race you to breakfast!"

Jade stared after her for a moment, and then, with a laugh that sounded suspiciously like a pixie's bell-like tones, she launched herself after the other pixie.

Buzzing her wings behind her in unison as fast as she could, she rocketed straight into the air, wobbled wildly, and flew hands first into a mushroom growing off the side of the pixie tree above her.

Pip's laugher echoed after her.

"Don't use all your wings at once." Pip landed on the

head of the mushroom above her and peered down at her through the petals. "Alternate, like a heartbeat. Back, then front, back, then front."

Jade screwed up her face, gathered her legs under her, and sprang into the air once more, careful this time to alternate the beating of her wings.

She rose higher and drifted forward, watching with delight as the ground dropped away beneath her, her flight much more controlled this time. It felt like nothing she had ever experienced before—so exhilarating!—and her wings beat faster just thinking about it, unbalancing her so that she wobbled a bit.

"Good!" Pip said, rising up next to her and coasting alongside her as she used her new control to fly forward. "Now suck your tummy in, hold your legs together straight out behind you, and put your arms forward as though you are diving into a lake."

Jade did as Pip said, and to her delight, the wobbling went away. "It works!" she said.

"Of course it works," Pip said.

Jade held her wings still, tilting them to catch the breeze, and she felt the air lift her and carry her forward—even better! The feel of the wind across her skin and through her hair was incredible. Flapping her wings slightly out of concert, she managed a tight spin, and then rose straight up to where Pip hovered.

"Nicely done!" Pip said. "Are you sure this is the first time you've flown?"

"Why can't I use all my wings at once?" Jade asked, carefully imitating Pip's wing movements to try to hold herself still in the air. At first she stuttered forward, then down, but after a moment, she got the hang of it. It was really like playing the drums back home—each different wing beat had a different rhythm, and each rhythm moved her in a different way.

"You can, but the closer you come to using your wings at the same time, the more powerful the thrust—making it very hard to control, especially for a new flyer," Pip said. "So just do it in emergencies, like when fleeing redcaps, or when playing stickyball, or when trying to get to the last sticky bun."

"Or when trying to beat you to breakfast?" Jade asked mischievously. And with that, she snapped her wings and took off, flapping as hard and fast as she could. She heard Pip take off after her, shrieking with delight.

Veering between trees, dodging pixies, skipping off the tops of unsuspecting elves' heads, Jade brought her wings as close to working in concert as she could without losing control. Pip was always right beside her, matching her wing stroke for wing stroke.

Scanning the ground, she caught sight of a swarm of pixies a short distance ahead, gathered around a long, wooden table piled high with giant, sugar-coated blackberries, frosted scones, and honey-coated sticky buns. The moment the table came into view, she saw Pip give an extra burst of speed.

Jade raised her wings and dived, baring her teeth in a grin. She rocketed toward the ground, brushing the soil with her fingertips before flapping hard—back wings first—to pull up and gently drift to the ground.

"I won! I won!" Jade said. "Gods, that was fun. I love flying."

Pip fluttered down, an envious look on her face. "Yeah, well, I wasn't really trying," Pip said, but she was grinning as she shouldered in among the other faeries to make two places for them at the table.

"Sure you weren't," Jade said. Pip handed her a plate and she filled it with sticky buns, pieces of berries, and an assortment of other sugar-coated goodies. Boy was she ravenous! She trembled all over. It must be the flying, she thought. Hungry work, flying.

By this time, the crowd of pixies had noticed them.

"Hey!" said one of them, a boy with a shock of light purple hair with green streaks and similar wings. "Pip! Are you going to introduce us to your friend?"

"Cousin Quinn, this," Pip said proudly around a mouthful of sticky bun, "is Vira Wyvernsting. A human!"

"She doesn't look like a human," Quinn said suspiciously,

and the other pixies murmured in agreement, some taking flight to get a better look.

"Yeah, humans don't fly!" said another pixie in a very high-pitched, fast voice, looking around for agreement. This pixie was small even by Jade's new standards. It had a tuft of blue hair and a body as round as a kitten's.

"She's not just a human, she's *the* human—the one from the glaistig's prophecy, with the locket," Pip said, pointing to the locket around Jade's neck. "And the pixie is her faerie form."

The faeries all buzzed with excitement and fluttered around Jade to get a good look at her and the locket.

"We're usually not taken very seriously," Pip explained. "No one expected the locket to turn the human girl into a pixie! An elf, maybe, or a satyr. I think the only reason the Sun King trusted me with bringing you the locket was because no one would suspect a pixie of being given such an important task, which means we can usually come and go as we please."

"So this is big," Jade surmised.

"Huge," Pip confirmed.

Jade wondered if this would raise suspicions at the Forever Court as to her true identity, but decided, with all Pip's gossipy relatives watching, that this would be a bad time to ask. She thought about how Pip had said that she would get in a lot of trouble if the Forever Court found out Jade wasn't Vira—and remembered how the Sun King had specifically requested her sister and not her. Perhaps this was one of the reasons why, not that her sister would be better than her, but that they didn't respect the pixies, and to have their human express kinship with a pixie would force them to respect the pixies more than they wanted to.

"I'm glad I'm the one you gave the locket to, and that I turned out to be a pixie," Jade said, hoping Pip took her meaning.

"So am I," Pip said, beaming.

Chapter Ten

After breakfast, Pip explained that she had chores to do. Chores. Even in the land of the faeries there were chores.

Jade begged for Pip to help her with her task instead. She just had to talk to the banshrae and figure out where to start looking for the queen's new source of magic. She still had no idea what to do, the faeries were all counting on her, and she was on her second day!

But the pixie was adamant. Chores had to be done. Otherwise there would be no sticky buns with their midday meal, and that would be a real disaster.

Finally, Jade decided to go with Pip in the hopes that maybe they could fly by the Forever Court on their way back. She was pretty sure she would need Pip's help in finding the banshrae. Besides, faerie chores couldn't possibly be as boring as human chores. She found it hard to believe that the pixie got down on her hands and knees and scrubbed anything.

She couldn't have been more right.

"Are all your chores this life threatening?" Jade panted, flying at a speed she wouldn't have dreamed possible that morning. In front of her, flying in a perfect circle formation, six pixies—including Pip and her cousin Quinn—used magic to keep a ball of honey spinning between them as a cloud of very angry, almost pixie-sized bees pursued them. The buzzing of wings was a roar. Pip was serving as the caller, which meant she flew in the back end of the circle so she could see where they were going and shouted out directions.

"If only!" Pip grinned. "On your left!"

Jade turned left, reached into the satchel she had been given, and lobbed a glue-filled stickyball at the bee that tried to cut in from her left. She was serving as floating defense, which meant she flew just behind the whole crew and fended off the bees that tried to disrupt the faerie circle and steal back their honey.

Seeing another bee coming from above, she lobbed a glitterbomb at it. The little pixie package exploded into sticky, bright, and blinding glitter.

Covered in glue, the bee spun out of control and hit a tree, where it stuck, buzzing and struggling to free itself, no longer a threat.

The faeries were still some distance from the pixie glen, but they had to lose the bees before they returned. Otherwise all the other pixies would be in danger. How exactly they intended to do that was beyond Jade. She hoped they didn't expect her to get rid of the bees all by herself. While her satchel held a great number of stickyballs, glitterbombs, and trick rope traps, it couldn't possibly hold enough to stop all the bees. And even if it did, those faeries would be waiting a long time if they expected her to glue each bee individually.

Looking to the right, she saw something that gave her an idea.

"Sharp right!" she called, and the honey circle turned the moment she got the words out. These faeries were practiced. She threw a pixie trick rope trap behind her, which quickly tied itself to two branches, catching two more bees and sending them spinning off course, giving the pixies some time to maneuver.

Ahead were the massive, mazelike funnel webs of the fiddleback spiders, the outer shells of which hardened into a substance as tough as bone, and the inner webs of which were the softest silk. The brownie at the Forever Court had told her about them when explaining where the spidersilk for their garments came from. According to the brownie, these spiders were as venomous as the red-vested bees, but not much of a danger if the pixies didn't get stuck in the webs.

"Tight formation!" Pip called. "This stuff is sticky!"

The honey circle pulled together as they approached the webs. And in seconds, they were flying through the neck of the funnel. Jade heard a series of *pops* as the vanguard of the bees slammed into the sticky webbing, like darts hitting a board, followed by the excited chittering and clicking of the oversized spiders sensing prey caught in their webs. Shadows fell over the group as the black, leggy spiders dropped down from above, blocking the entrance even more.

Then, the next wave of bees approached, only to be confronted with hungry spiders. Jade grinned, looking behind her at the befuddled bees, clearly out of their league with the larger, more dangerous spiders. That should take care of their pursuers.

"Ha!" Jade said as they flew out of the tunnel and into the open air. "We did it!"

"No, you did it," Pip said, grinning.

"We did it," Jade said firmly, returning Pip's grin.

"Pip, Jade, look," said Reeva, one of the other pixies. Jade looked around. The part of the forest they had emerged in glittered under a thick coat of ice. The other faeries all stopped their chatting and went silent as stones as they looked at the wintry landscape.

"The Ice Queen," Jade said, flying closer to the nearest outcropping of ice.

"This is closer than they've ever been before," Pip said, following close behind. "This is getting bad."

"I told you we should have gone looking for the queen's magic this morning!" Jade whispered. A strange sound echoed her words, like a hissing sigh. Jade cocked her head to listen, but the sound seemed to have stopped. Oh no. What if the winter faeries weren't gone yet? What if the Ice Queen was just past those trees? She wasn't ready yet, not to face the queen. Frost had said she'd need a plan. Phoenix had had a plan and failed, and Jade didn't have a plan, and Jade most certainly wasn't Phoenix.

"What good is trying to save the world on an empty stomach?" Pip said. "We need food if we're going to—"

"Shhh," Jade said. She strained her ears for the sound she'd heard before. One way or another, she had to know what was on the other side of those trees. That was what she was here for. "I think I hear something."

The pixies all held as silent as they could, the only sound the ever-present buzzing of their wings. Then it happened again: a long, raspy intake of breath, the telltale sign of a dragon about to unleash its ultimate weapon.

"It's coming from over there!" Jade whispered, motioning the faeries quietly forward so that Pip, at one side of the ring surrounding the honey, was closest to her, and Quinn farthest away. They flew over to one of the few trees that was not encased in ice and peeked between the large, olive green leaves.

In the clearing before her, she saw four young white dragons, each about the size of a pony, with scales the blue-white iridescent color of ice when the sun hits it. They sat with their wings folded around them like capes. The forest around them in almost all directions was frozen solid.

Just then, one of the dragons took a great, raspy breath and let it out, freezing a large section of trees, birds still in their branches.

"What does this mean?" Jade whispered, confused.

"I don't know," Pip whispered. "But I bet it's important. Aren't you glad you came with me now?"

"What are you guys talking about?" Quinn asked. "What do you see?"

"None of your business, prissy wings!" Pip called back. "Quiet down," Jade said. "They'll hear us."

"What do you mean, 'none of my business'!" Quinn shouted, his high pixie voice ringing through the clearing. Jade winced, holding her ears. At first, nothing seemed to happen. She held her breath.

"Oh no," Quinn whispered as he caught sight of the dragons. "There are so many. Why are there so many . . ."

All of the dragons swiveled their heads to where the pixies were hovering, their cold black eyes focusing in on Jade, and their jaws opening in anticipation. One of them gave a fierce cry that sounded like a cross between a wildcat and a hunting hawk. Three of them thundered across the clearing, drawing in breath, while the fourth, who had a puckered scar across its right eye, beat its wings and rose up out of the clearing, soaring quickly out of sight. For a moment, Jade was frozen in awe at the sight. Then she found her voice.

"Back through the spider tunnels, quick!" Jade cried. "Fly!"

She could hear the dragons behind them, breaking branches and crushing roots. A rush of frosty air flew right over Jade's head and slicked the tree in front over her with ice so thick she couldn't see the bark underneath.

Dodging the snapping jaws of another dragon, she beat her wings as fast as she could, struggling to stay ahead of the ice and teeth and claws. Then when she caught sight of the spider tunnel below, she raised her wings and dived as fast as she knew how, just as she had at breakfast.

She flew past the forest in a blur and shot right through the entrance to the tunnel, followed quickly by Pip and the rest of the pixies, who, upon reaching the inside of the tunnel, erupted in cheering.

"Whew," she panted. "That was—"

But before she could finish her sentence, frosty air slammed into the tunnel entrance, sealing it off with ice. She flew over to the ice, putting her hands on it without thinking, and drew them back with a hiss. The ice was colder than normal! Her hands felt numb already.

The celebratory shouts of the faeries behind her turned to screams. She turned back around and shrieked. A spider was right in front of her, dividing her from her friends.

Hovering, careful to avoid touching the web in the narrow tunnel, she backed up very slowly as the spider reared up on its hind legs. Its mandibles were huge—as big as her feet at least. It lunged, and she dodged out of the way just in time. She heard the snapping of its teeth and saw its legs punch through the webbing where she had been a moment before. She saw it struggle to free its legs from the tangling threads.

And that gave her an idea.

Chapter Eleven

With a couple quick shakes, she dumped the stickyballs out of her knapsack down the funnel.

"Come and get me!" she cried. The spider lurched immediately upon hearing her voice, ripping its feet from the web and charging down at her with astonishing speed, all eight legs moving in a rush. Flying as fast as she dared in the confining, sticky passage, and praying she didn't run into any other spiders, she flew back over the sticky path she had wrought. The spider charged after her, then stopped suddenly as its feet caught in the webbing. She saw the webbing of the funnel shaking around her.

Turning, she saw the spider struggle to free its caught legs, only to plunge its remaining legs through waiting stickyballs, splashing glue everywhere and effectively gluing its feet to the web. Before long, the spider was completely glued down.

"Maybe next time, spidey!" she called, waving as she flew over it. It gnashed its mandibles angrily and glared at her with its beady black eyes.

Just beyond that spider was another, but this one's back was to her as it menaced the circle. The faeries squealed and cried and tried to speed the other way, but another spider dropped down and guarded the exit, so they were stuck, dodging attacks from both sides, trying to stay away from the webbing, and struggling to keep the honey afloat. One faerie had already fallen prey to the webbing. The others tried valiantly to distract the spiders, but it was only a matter of time.

Without even thinking, Jade launched herself at the spider's back as it reared back for another stab at her friends. Swinging her satchel, she caught the bag part over the spider's head just as it lunged. Then, swinging her legs around its slender middle and holding tight, she pulled back sharply, wedging the bag in the spider's mouth. Confused, the spider reared again, and she pulled down and back sharply again, forcing the spider back to the ground. Just like riding a pony back home.

"Get behind me!" she cried.

"Vira Wyvernsting!" Pip cried upon seeing her. "Davin needs help!" But the faeries all flew as fast as they could to get behind her. Jade could feel the spider struggling underneath her, trying to attack the faeries as they swept right past it.

As soon as the last faerie was safely behind her, she loosened the satchel and kicked the spider in the abdomen, letting out a loud cry. Startled, the spider charged forward—straight at the other spider. The other spider let out a startled hiss and scrambled backward out of the funnel just as fast as its legs would carry it, Jade on her spider in hot pursuit.

"Davin, grab on!" she said, holding out her hand as she passed the faerie stuck in the web. Davin grasped her hand. The spider rushed onward, pulling Davin free of the web with a *pop*, and Jade swung him up behind her on the spider's back.

The faeries let out a cheer and flew out of the funnel into the open, where the spiders could not follow. "Davin, jump!" Jade cried, as they approached the end of the funnel at a fantastic pace. Abandoning the knapsack, they leaped off the spider's back and flew after the jubilant faerie circle.

"Wow, Vira Wyvernsting, good thinking! Fast too!" Pip said after they'd gotten back and spun the honey into the empty bottles they had prepared for it. "We'll tell stories about that for years."

"Are you kidding me?" said Quinn angrily, pulling an iridescent bubble filled with smoke out of his satchel. "She almost got us killed. First by dragons, then by spiders—all to escape a couple bees! How is that good thinking?" He threw the ball up and caught it.

"I was only trying to help," Jade said defensively. But a little knot of guilt gnawed at her. "How else was I supposed to get us away from the dragons?"

"She should never have been allowed to help with harvesting honey. That's for the bravest, cleverest, most experienced pixies only!" Quinn said, ignoring her question. What was it with faeries ignoring her? "We could all be frozen or eaten by now!"

"Yeah, well, we aren't, are we?" Pip said, sticking out her chin. "Besides, you're the one who made all the noise and attracted the dragons' attention."

"Only because you two were being so secretive!"

"Only because there were dragons!"

"She should have warned me! I should have been floating defense. I would have warned you," Quinn said. "She's not even a proper pixie."

"You take that back!" said Pip. Jade was surprised at the fervor in the pixie's voice. It was true, she wasn't a proper pixie. She didn't particularly see what got Pip so upset. "You're only saying that because she's not *your* human."

"She saved my life," Davin said quietly.

"It wouldn't have needed saving if she hadn't put your life in danger in the first place," Quinn said, keeping his glare focused on Pip.

"Yeah, well, if you hadn't—" Pip began, and Quinn threw the bubble at Pip. It exploded in a shower of smoke, and suddenly, Pip's mouth was moving, but no sound came out.

"I've had about enough your excuses!" Quinn said.

"Pip!" Jade cried, flying over to the furiously shouting yet curiously silent pixie. Pip's tongue, she noticed, was tied in a complex knot. Jade turned on Quinn, her hands balled into fists and her eyes hard. "What have you done to her?" Quinn just smirked at her. "Tell me what you've done!" Jade couldn't let Pip be hurt for defending her.

"She's fine," Davin said. "That's one of Quinn's silence bombs. It will wear off in a minute or so."

"Pip! Quinn!" called Reeva, who looked older and more experienced than either of the quarrelsome pixies. Reeva flew front guard, which meant she had to fly backward the entire time—quite a feat of flying and as such she was technically in charge.

The two pixies quieted immediately. Or rather, Quinn did—Pip was already quiet. "As you both know, there's only one way to resolve this," she said grimly. "Trial by sticky-ball. Pip, you're captain of one team. Quinn, you captain the other."

Fine! mouthed Pip, snapping to attention. *I pick Vira Wyvernsting.* It was the first time Jade had ever been picked first for anything, and even if it was by her sister's name, she felt her cheeks grow warm.

"I didn't say you could go first," Reeva admonished.

"That's just fine," Quinn snapped, ignoring Reeva as he stood nose to nose with Pip. "You can have her!

Who ever heard of a human who could play stickyball? I pick Reeva."

"Pip?" Jade whispered. "What are the rules to this stickyball?"

Rules? the pixie mouthed.

Chapter Twelve

Stickyball, as it turned out, was something like dodgeball, only you played with stickyballs instead of normal balls. There was no court, no out of bounds, and no rules. The last team with a player still able to fly—despite all the stuff that inevitably ended up stuck all over you—won.

Tactically, Jade was nothing like the more experienced faeries, but she was a pretty good shot and a natural at flying. So far, she had only an acorn and half a pansy stuck to her.

Quinn, of course, had made her his primary target from the very beginning. But having expected that, Pip had taken after him with a vengeance, and Jade had been able to dodge him and find a place to hide next to the pile of stickyballs used for restocking.

She peered out from behind the mushroom. The coast seemed clear. Then she heard labored beating of wings and ducked quickly back under the mushroom. A faerie flew low toward the restocking pile, struggling under the weight of the angry, chattering shimmerling stuck to his butt.

Ah, it was just Davin, one of her teammates.

She left the safety of the mushroom and was just about to call out Davin's name when Quinn came hurtling down from above, lobbing stickyballs at Davin.

Davin let out a squawk and scrambled to get out of the path of fire, but he was just too awkward with that other faerie stuck to his butt! Not to mention he glowed bright as a fallen star with that shimmerling attached to him!

He was going to need help.

Jade dashed out from her cover, and as she flew toward Quinn's unprotected left flank, she saw Pip come out from Quinn's right flank. Her clever idea suddenly seemed a lot less clever—everyone had been lying in wait at the restocking zone? Really?

Jade shivered. It was unusually cold for a spring day. She must have been sitting still too long. Nothing a little stickyball couldn't cure!

Letting out a loud battle cry, Jade threw her remaining two stickyballs—only to see them freeze in midair, coated in a thick skin of ice.

The frozen stickyballs shattered as they hit the ground, sending shards of cloudy, frozen glue everywhere.

Quinn looked at her and cursed. But then everyone's attention was drawn downward. Another icy shot flew

116

through the air and hit Davin. In an instant, the pixie and the shimmerling were both encased entirely in ice.

They fell and hit the ground with a resounding *thud*.

"Davin!" Jade cried.

The ice moved toward Jade like a wave. Sparse flakes of snow began to fall, just like when the redcaps had appeared. Her locket felt like ice on her chest.

And then she heard the sound of wings, and snow swirled around her as a white dragon with a puckered scar across its right eye and an elf astride its back landed in the clearing. Jade recognized the dragon—it was the same dragon who had fled the clearing earlier.

Cold air emanated from the elf riding the dragon. Her hair was black as ink, and her eyes were solid, reflective silver—just like the elves that were training her sister. The Moonsing Archers, right?

The elf put a hand on the back of the white dragon's neck, and the dragon cracked open its jaws, leaking frost and a cloud of wintry air.

She stroked the dragon's neck, and the dragon curled its neck toward her, though its eyes remained alert.

"Ah, pixies," the elf said. "You all look alike to me. Tell me: which one of you is Jade? I have a birthday present for you, and I'd hate to give it to the wrong person."

"Go home to your queen, winter faerie!" Reeva said as the pixies all formed in what Jade now knew was a battle formation. They were being very brave, Jade thought, going up against an elf and a dragon. "You're not welcome here in the land of the Sun King."

"I'll give you a hint," the elf said, ignoring Reeva. "Which one of you wears the locket?"

"Pip?" Quinn said, turning accusing eyes on the pixie. "Do you know what she's talking about?"

Pip looked around guiltily. "No."

"Really?" the elf said. "What a pity." She didn't sound sorry at all. With a flick of her wrist, she directed the dragon toward Pip. "I guess I'll just have to freeze the lot of you. Rimewind? If you would—"

"Pip, it's no use!" Jade cried, ready to give herself up.

"No, *Vira Wyvernsting*," Pip said. "This is important."

"Vira Wyvernsting, eh?" The elf smirked and both she and the dragon turned to look at Jade. "I think I've figured out your riddle."

"Naomi, stop," a stern voice commanded. Jade turned and saw the voice belonged to the Sun Prince, who was walking toward them, his hands held behind his back.

Beside him strode the banshrae. What were they doing here so soon after the arrival of the elf, who Jade realized now was a winter faerie. How did the Sun Prince know the elf's name?

"Ah, Frost! Your mother sends her fondest greetings,"

Naomi said. "You really should come visit more often. She gets so cold and lonely when you are away."

"Go home," the Sun Prince said sternly. "Now is not the time for this."

The elf laughed, a harsh, manic sound like breaking glass.

Jade looked from the prince to the elf. Not the time for what exactly? Surely they weren't working together.

"Now is the perfect time for this!" Naomi scoffed.

"I'm warning you," Frost said. "Don't make me hurt you."

"I'd like to see you try," the elf sneered, and she directed the white dragon at Frost. "Rimewind, attack—"

But before she could finish, the Sun Prince's hands came out from behind his back, and glittering, yellow dust that smelled of rose with underlying jasmine, cinnamon, and strawberries flew out. The petals' pollen—sparkling so brightly she could see the enchantment on it!

Jade held her breath and flew out of the enchanted cloud as quickly as she was able. The other pixies were not so quick and fell like rocks, asleep as soon as the potent pollen hit them.

"What trick is . . . " the elf began before she and Rimewind, too, collapsed to the ground, snoring softly. The prince smiled coldly.

"I warned you," he said, looking down at the slumbering elf and dragon, standing well out of the cloud of enchanted pollen as it settled to the ground.

"Petal dust," Jade said, flying down to hover just above Frost's head. "You enchanted pollen from the petals to put them all to sleep." The prince's head shot up.

"Vira Wyvernsting?" Frost said, squinting and catching sight of the locket around her neck. "The locket turned you into a pixie." He shook his head. "I should have known," he said, brushing the rest of the petal dust off his hands.

"What's that supposed to mean?" Jade demanded. "And what are you doing here anyway?" And more important, what was he doing here so soon after the arrival of the winter faerie?

"Saving you," Frost said, frowning.

But that didn't make any sense. He hadn't even known she was there until just now.

"What are *you* doing here?" Frost said. "You're playing pixie games when you have only a day and a half left to find the new source of the queen's magic? I thought you were going to help us stop this war."

"I wasn't playing, I . . ." Jade's heart sank. The prince was right.

But what was she supposed to have done?

She had gotten no guidance at all from him or anyone else. The only one who had said he'd help her at all had been the banshrae, who was supposedly the Sun King's right hand. She looked over at Aron, willing him to say something directly into her head like last time, but he was studiously ignoring her.

"You're lucky I came along," Frost said. "If I hadn't, you'd be nothing more than an icy snack for Naomi."

"I could have managed," she said, turning away from the banshrae to glare at him. She'd defeated the redcaps, a spriggan, a glaistig—all right, she'd left on her own account but still—bees, white dragons, and some really nasty spiders on her own, hadn't she?

"Doubtful. The only way you would have survived is if Naomi had some use for you," Frost said. He looked down at the elf with something like regret. "She is very skilled at what she does. I didn't really want to hurt her. I used to know her. I used to . . . like her. But at the end of the day, she has to obey her orders, doesn't she." He seemed bitter about that. Jade wondered if it had something to do with the "I used to like her" bit. Maybe he used to *like* her, like her. That might explain the attitude. "What I want to know is how the Ice Queen found out about you—and figured out which faerie you were before we did."

"So everyone knew I was going to turn into a faerie before I did," Jade said.

"A human is vulnerable in the Feywild—a faerie less so," Frost said. "It makes you harder to track as you look . . . considerably different. Still, I didn't think you'd be a pixie. An elf maybe, or a dryad." Sure, the pretty faeries,

Jade thought, like my pretty sister. "Something that could lift a sword, at least, and be of some use."

"Pixies are brave," Jade said. She remembered what Pip had said about the lack of respect pixies garnered in the Forever Court. "And clever."

"Whatever," Frost said. "There's nothing we can do about it now, anyway."

Frost turned and picked up Davin carefully. Jade's wings buzzed a little quicker. "Where are you taking him?" Poor Davin had a horrified expression on his face. She wondered if he'd be frozen for all time, like Phoenix. It had all happened so quickly. One minute, Davin had been playing stickyball, and the next, he was a sculpture. And it had been all her fault. If she hadn't been with them, if she had been doing her job like she was supposed to, not playing with the pixies, Davin would still be safe.

"Aron?" Frost said. "Take Naomi back to the castle. Bind her and wait for me in the library. I won't be long." Maybe once the prince left, she could go with Aron and ask him about what he'd said earlier, about helping her. She tried to catch Aron's eye, but Aron just nodded at Frost and moved silently over to the elf.

Frost turned back to Jade. "You, come with me. I'll need your help."

Jade started to follow then stopped. Why would Frost

want her to come with him when up until now, he'd been so dismissive?

She saw the prince looking at Aron, and she narrowed her eyes. Of course. The prince had stopped her from talking to the banshrae before, at the dance. Now he was doing it again. Somehow he'd figured out that the banshrae wanted to help her, and he didn't want her to be the one to help the Sun King. He wanted to do it himself—for her to "stay out of it." She sighed. She hated it when people treated her as if they were better off without her, as if she'd just be in the way—like her sister did. She could help! She would have to prove she could help. She had to come up with an excuse to get away from him and talk to Aron.

"I can't. What about my friends?" she protested.

"Petal pollen holds sleeping enchantments particularly well—and this batch was freshly ensorcelled. With the amount the dragon got, he should be out for the rest of the day," Frost said, his hand closing over Davin's form a little tighter. "Your friends are safe."

Not *all* her friends were safe, Frost's hands seemed to say. Davin was in Frost's hands. Frost, who didn't want her to talk to the only faerie who had offered to help her. Frost, who had taken Davin hostage. If she wanted to make sure Davin was safe, she was going to have to go along. She'd have to find Aron later.

"Are you coming or not? Make your decision quickly if you want him to live," Frost said. She felt a flutter of hope in her chest. So there was a cure! Or at least, that was what he wanted her to believe. "On the other hand, if you don't want him to live, you have all the time in the world."

"Of course I want him to live," Jade snapped. She might not be responsible for getting Davin killed after all.

"Well then?" Frost said. The prince's flesh turned red where it touched Davin's frozen form. Jade remembered the ice from the spiders' caves and how her fingers had gone numb just from touching it for an instant. How much worse was it for Davin inside the ice? It might be a trick, she knew. There might not be a cure. This might be her only chance to talk to Aron alone. But what choice did she have? If it weren't for her, Davin wouldn't be frozen at all. She made her decision.

"All right, fine," Jade said. "I'm going with you."

"Good," Frost said, turning to leave.

"It's not for you, though," Jade said to his back. "It's for Davin."

"Come on, then. We have to move quickly," Frost said, setting off at a brisk walk. "We have only a short time in which to treat him before the frost makes its way to his heart."

Pumping her wings, she flew after him. *I'll find you later*, she thought at the banshrae, just in case he could hear her. *Right now, I have a job to do.*

Chapter Thirteen

Jade followed Frost into the main hall of the Forever Court and through a door hidden behind the thrones, then up a tight, winding staircase punctuated with tiny, pixie-sized doors—servant corridors, he explained, cementing her understanding of the place of pixies in the Forever Court.

Finally, they came to a magnificent golden door with carved dragons on either side—dragons that looked vaguely familiar. But how could they look familiar when she'd never been here before?

The dragons began to stir as Frost and Jade approached, their stony wings clicking and grinding. Her locket began to glow, illuminating the dragons as though they were on fire! Suddenly it came back to her. These were the same dragons as she'd seen in her vision in the punchbowl at the Forever Court. But what did it mean?

The Sun Prince murmured something too softly for her to hear into the ear of each carved dragon, and they quieted. Her locket, however, still glowed.

She stared at the dragons. They're guards to prevent us from breaking in, she realized. But why would she have visions about that? She logged it in the back of her mind just in case she ever felt a need to break into secret palace rooms.

Frost traced his fingers over the carvings on the door, pressed in first a rose, then a sun, and then a stag.

"What is this place?" Jade said. With so many safeguards and such a fancy door, it must be a treasury or something.

"This is my room," the Sun Prince said as the door shuddered and then slowly evaporated into mist.

"With all that protection?" Jade said, thinking of her little bunk back home. The prince gave her a crooked smiled.

"There's a war on," the prince said dryly. "You can't be too careful." He gestured into the room. "Come. The items we need are in here."

Jade followed him into the room, starting when the door materialized again behind them. The prince led her past an assortment of wonders—paintings, jewels, crowns, and strange mechanical devices. On the far side of the room stood an expansive, four-poster bed carved of a ghostly gray-white wood. Around it, gauzy sapphire curtains laced with crystals caught the light. Next to the bed was an elf-sized wardrobe carved from similarly white wood and etched with silver.

Frost walked directly to the wardrobe, opened the door, and pushed aside a mess of princely garments made out of all manner of fabrics. Jade flew up to hover over his shoulder and watched as he knelt to remove a false panel from the bottom of the wardrobe. Underneath, he carefully drew out a pair of elaborate hand mirrors—one gold and the other silver—from their velvet and silk wrappings. Her locket blazed like a bonfire as soon as they were unveiled.

Jade swooped closer to get a better look and gasped.

"What are those?" she asked. The mirrors did not reflect the interior of the room. Instead, inside the silver one, a room filled with ice, snow, and dark-looking relics awaited. Inside the gold one was a room filled with fire, flowers, and cunning artifacts too bright to look at.

"These are how we're going to save Davin," Frost said.

"Mirrors?" she said doubtfully. "It's not like he needs his hair done or something." He looked at her scornfully, and she noticed that her locket was still glowing, throwing large shadows against the walls.

"Touch your locket and repeat after me," Frost said. *"Alrhys rahv iislira."*

Jade put a hand over her locket and looked at Frost dubiously. *"Alrhys rahv iislira,"* she said, and noticed with awe that the mirrors both began to pulse with light in time with her locket. Their surfaces shimmered and crawled as though they were made of beetles. "What's going on?" Jade asked. "What did I do?"

"Touch the silver mirror," Frost said.

"Why?" Jade asked. "Tell me what's going on, or I'm not doing anything!"

"Do you want to save him or not?" Frost said.

"Yes, but—"

"Then touch the mirror!"

Jade flew down to the mirror. He nodded impatiently. Taking a deep breath, she pressed her fingers to the mirror's surface.

The silvery metal stuck to her fingers. Gasping, she tried to pull away, but the silver metal rushed up the skin of her arms, quickly enveloping her. There was a flash of brilliant light as it hit her locket. A cold, clinging wave passed up her body, pressing in with almost unbearable force, sending shivers up and down her spine and taking her breath away.

And then the feeling was gone.

She found herself in a large room made of ice. Carved shelves adorned the walls, and snow fell softly from somewhere above. She could not see the ceiling.

She could see the prince on the other side of the mirror, reflected in the mirror's surface.

Oh no—he'd tricked her. He'd pulled her through to the other side of the mirror, and now she was trapped!

"Frost!" Jade yelped. "Let me out of here! Frost!"

Through the mirror, she saw him mouth something, and he touched his fingers to the mirror. She backed up as a thin line of liquid silver spun its way out of the mirror and wove around the prince's shape like spiders weaving a web.

Then Frost was inside the frosty room too.

The look he gave her was slightly amused and belittling all at once.

Jade felt her face flush. "What is that thing?" she asked quickly to cover her embarrassment.

"It's a long story," the Sun Prince said, his smile dropping away. He placed Davin, still glowing with the light of the shimmerling, on an icy table.

"So . . . tell me," Jade pushed.

The prince sighed. His breath steamed in the wintry air like a white dragon's breath weapon.

"The mirror we're in is my mother's trove," Frost said. "See . . ." —he paused for a moment, then ran his hand through his hair—"Phoenix and I were the ones who stole the troves."

"What!" Jade gasped. That's what the vision about the dragons must have meant—it was pointing out the location of the troves. "But that's not what you said—"

"I know what I said," Frost snapped before taking a deep breath. "Look, no one can know what we did. Please"—he sounded as though the word didn't come easy to him—"we were only trying to help. We stole both troves, and sealed them so that they could only be opened if the locket, worn by a human, were present, and the special pass phrase uttered. The human part was Phoenix's idea—a last safeguard against betrayal, should the locket fall into the wrong hands. She alone had the locket, and I alone had the pass phrase. We were going to confront the Sun King and Ice Queen together, ending the war before anyone got hurt. But it didn't go the way I planned . . ."

"Obviously," Jade said before she could stop herself. She clapped her hands over her mouth.

"Look," the Sun Prince said, eyeing her frostily. "The only reason I didn't tell you sooner is that there were all those other faeries around. You have to believe me. Don't tell anyone, all right?"

"All right. I won't tell," Jade said. "But what happened?"

The prince walked over to one of the shelves and took down a partially filled crystal vial. Inside the vial, a single blue-white spark floated amid a clear liquid.

"Phoenix changed the plan," Frost said.

Frost set the uncorked vial next to Davin and turned back to the shelves.

"When I woke up, Phoenix was already gone," Frost continued, running his fingers along ornate metal boxes, glowing orbs, swords made of black ice, and the other cruel-looking objects on the shelves. "All she left was a note, telling me what she'd done."

He paused, his hands closing around a long box carved of yellow-white bone. Jade held her breath, careful not to interrupt.

"I couldn't believe it, that she'd leave me alone like that. That she could be so selfish. We'd said that whatever we ended up doing, we'd do it together. That we'd always be there for each other, no matter what happened." The prince put the ivory box down on the icy table with enough force to splash himself and her both in snow. He seemed not to notice. "And then, she had to go off and leave me to try to defeat the Ice Queen."

"Why did she do it?" Jade asked, watching as Frost opened the box, revealing a long, glistening wand carved of what looked like glass nestled among countless layers blue silk. On the base was an engraving. Jade swooped to take a closer look. It was an iron rose. What did that mean?

"She said she did it because she believed in second chances, but I think she just didn't think I could stand up to Mother," the prince said bitterly. "If only she'd trusted me. She wouldn't have been frozen in the first place if I had been there with her.

"Now you understand why no one else can know about this," Frost said. "If my father knew we stole the troves, he'd just take his trove back and use it to destroy my mother."

"How do you know that?" Jade asked.

"I know my parents," Frost said bitterly. "After Phoenix was frozen, my father went to the glaistig for help, and she gave him that prophecy and the locket—Phoenix must have given it to her before she confronted the Ice

Queen—escalating things again." Frost looked deep into her eyes, and Jade felt herself holding her breath. "You have to help me figure out how the Ice Queen is still using her magic. We have to fix this before they find out what Phoenix and I did, before they destroy each other, just like they destroyed Phoenix."

"You sound like you really cared about her," Jade said softly. "Was she your girlfriend or something?"

"No," Frost said. "She was my sister."

The implications hit Jade like a slap to the face. "The Ice Queen froze her own daughter?" she exclaimed. And she got angry when her mother sent her to bed without dessert. "That's awful!"

"Well, Phoenix wasn't exactly what you'd call diplomatic," the prince said. "My mother isn't evil—she just needs to be handled a certain way, otherwise she gets angry. And Phoenix was the worst person for that job. No one was supposed to get hurt. Not Phoenix, not my father, and not my mother. I was supposed to be there with Phoenix to talk to Mother. I can't help but think if I had been there, this never would have happened."

"Wait," Jade said, her mind reeling. "Are you actually defending her?"

"She's not evil," Frost repeated. "It's just that no one understands her. No one except me, anyway. Now, if you'll excuse me, I have to focus on this part."

Jade's mind reeled. Phoenix was Frost's sister, and they were both the children of the Ice Queen and the Sun King. Frost's sister was frozen, his father was powerless, and his mother was out to destroy them all—but he loved her anyway. No wonder he was so moody all the time.

Jade was no longer worried about him trying to force her out. Now she was worried that his love for his mother blinded him to the fact that the queen was crazy. He still seemed to think that she could be saved, that everything would be all right. And no wonder: even after she'd frozen his sister, he was unable to condemn her.

Jade was too lost in thought to worry about what the prince was or was not about to do when he picked up the icy wand. This was so much more complicated than she had initially thought. She had thought that learning about Phoenix would give her the answers, but it only raised more questions.

Putting one end of the wand on Davin, the prince murmured to himself. The wand began to glow a bright white, flickering with sapphire blue flames. Winter magic. The prince was using winter magic! But before she could protest, the ice encasing Davin began to melt into a puddle of blue-white ooze that nosed around the table like a curious snail. Keeping the wand on the faerie, Frost used his free hand to pour the contents of the vial on the accumulating ooze. Jade watched in fascination as the spark flowed out of the vial and into the ooze, where it lent the whole liquid its wintry glow.

As soon as the ice melted off the faerie entirely, Frost abandoned Davin and used both his free hand and the wand to cast another spell—this one spinning the liquid up like the pixies spun honey, only with a magic as white as snow, sending it back into the vial. As soon as it filled the vial, he capped it. The bottle was completely full.

After replacing the vial on the shelf, Frost returned his wand to the very still form of Davin.

Reluctantly, Jade turned her attention to his task as well and was immediately hit by a wave of shame. The prince had been focusing all his attention on saving one of her friends, one she had gone along solely to protect, and she had stopped thinking about Davin entirely.

"Come on," Frost murmured, using the wand to siphon the cold out of the faerie's tiny body in a stream of miniscule snowflakes. Jade watched, holding her breath. She wasn't sure she could forgive herself if Davin had been killed because of her.

Why hadn't she given herself up, anyway? The winter faerie Naomi was clearly after her. She had even used her real name.

Speaking of which, how had Naomi learned her real name? Moreover, would the prince get it from the elf when he questioned her and find out Jade was a fraud? Fear of being caught pulled at her again, but then Davin gasped, taking his first free breath, and sat up.

The glue failed to hold through the stress of both the movement and the cold, and he pulled free of the shimmerling. Jade immediately forgot her fears and let out a giant sigh of relief.

"It worked," Frost said, a fleeting smile crossing his face.

"You weren't sure?" Jade exclaimed, casting a startled glance over her shoulder as she flew down to Davin.

"I've never had a chance to try it before." The prince shrugged, watching her and Davin with a strange expression on his face.

Jade took hold of Davin's hand. It was clammy and cold, but she could feel his heart beat. His eyes stared sightlessly ahead for a moment before focusing on her. Then he smiled.

"You saved me," Davin said. "Again."

"No, the prince saved you. I'm just the one who nearly got you killed," Jade said, hugging his limp form. "Again."

"Ha. Don't let Pip hear you say that," Davin said, his voice seeming to come from a long way away. Then his eyes rolled back in his head and he passed out again. Jade started, but was relieved to see that his chest rose and fell regularly. He was just asleep. She patted his hand. He was even warming up.

"He should be fine in a few hours," Frost said. "I've drawn all the winter out of him."

"Thank you," Jade said seriously, standing up and flying to hover in front of Frost's nose. "But why show me all this? Why tell me about Phoenix? You wanted nothing to do with my help last night."

"Because I want you to trust me," Frost said.

"Yes, but why?" Jade said.

"We're in a war," Frost said, staring into her eyes intently. "And it's not just winter versus summer. If you really want to help me, if you really want to stop this war, then we need to work together. And that means you'll have to trust me no matter what anyone—even the Sun King himself—says. Can I depend on you to do that?"

Jade fidgeted, uncomfortable with the direction of the conversation. While she was grateful to the prince for his help with Davin and felt sorry for Frost for getting in between his parents' war, she found she agreed with Phoenix. The Sun Prince was far too softhearted when it came to the Ice Queen. He simply couldn't be trusted.

Frost waited, watching her closely. He still held the glass wand, almost forgotten by her side. Or that was just what she was supposed to think?

"Why can't we just work together?" Jade asked, feeling awkward and out of place. Vira was so much better at this kind of thing.

"Because," Frost said, his voice soft but firm, as though he were talking to a frightened kitten. "I need to know I can depend on you. You're not going to tell anyone about me and Phoenix, are you?"

"I already said I wouldn't!" Jade snapped.

"Then what is the problem?" Frost demanded. "I need to know you're going to help us—me. Not fight against me." Us. The prince still spoke as though his sister were alive and working with him, as though the Ice Queen hadn't frozen his sister, as though their plan still had a chance of working.

Flying over to the shelves, Jade made a show of looking over the strange and wicked-looking magical creations that were almost carelessly heaped upon the icy shelves.

"There's just one other thing I still don't understand," Jade said. "If you can save Davin, why didn't you save Phoenix?"

"She's been frozen a long time," the prince said, sounding a bit annoyed at the direction the conversation had taken. He tapped the glass wand in the palm of his hand. Jade didn't like the ease and familiarity with which he handled such an icy wand, the way his fingers seemed to itch to use it again, even if it *had* saved Davin. "So unfreezing her would require more than just manipulating the existing winter magic—it would require powerful summer magic, and I don't do summer magic. Look, I need to know if I can trust you—"

"But you could still try!" Jade pressed, cutting him off. "And what about if you gave the Sun King back his magic and got him to help you? Phoenix is all alone out there, in the cold, far away from the Forever Court."

"Because then the Sun King would use his magic to escalate the war with the Ice Queen again, making things even worse than they are now," the prince said sharply. "Don't you understand? I don't want anyone else to get hurt, and my parents, they can't be trusted to do that. That's why it's so important that you work with me and not my father."

"But she's your sister!" Jade said. "And surely between the both of you, you could confess to your parents what you did and they would see what a mistake they'd made in starting a war and forcing you two onto different sides, and–"

"No," Frost said. "It wouldn't work out like that."

"Why not? How do you know?" Jade said.

"I don't have time for this," Frost said. "Give me an answer: yes or no."

Jade turned to look at the prince, her brow furrowed.

"But the Ice Queen–" Jade began.

"Didn't you hear me?" the prince said, his voice growing sharp. "Answer me!"

"But this could–" Jade started, certain that if she could just get the prince to listen . . .

"Go!" the prince snapped, his sapphire eyes blazing. "I should have known better than to expect you to understand. Just take your friends and go!" A wintry glow erupted along the wand as if in response to his anger, magic swirling around it like drifts of snow.

"All right, fine!" Jade said, backing up and pulling Davin and the shimmerling with her. Her heart beat against her ribs like a caged bird. "I'm going!" She'd finally pushed him too far. He was going to freeze her, just like the Ice Queen froze his sister. Why hadn't she just promised him she'd do what he said, that she'd work with him? At least that way she'd have an ally, and maybe learn something useful. Now he was going to do everything in his power to thwart her.

The last thing Jade observed before the cold pressure of the mirror consumed her, was that Frost was muttering to himself again: "Stupid pixies."

Chapter Fourteen

Jade didn't remember much about how she got out of the castle or how she had gotten so far beyond it into the ancient forest beyond. She had vague memories of getting Davin back to his tree, and she knew the shimmerling had wandered off at some point, but aside from that . . .

She just couldn't get the image of Frost out of her head—his blue eyes hard as ice, that awful wand blazing with winter magic, him defending his mother despite everything. The scene kept replaying in her head as she turned the locket over and over again, trying to find the hidden catch that would let its secrets loose.

But the locket, and the scene, remained cold, smooth, and closed to her. So she drifted deeper into the woods, still turning the locket and the scene, until all around her were trees with black bark and long, dripping beards of tangled green moss. The canopy was thick enough to block out the sun, and the only light came from phosphorescent green mushrooms that grew like pimples on the faces of some of the younger trees.

Everything made sense, almost. Frost and Phoenix wanted their parents to stop fighting, so they stole their magic. But everything went terribly wrong when Phoenix confronted the Ice Queen alone and ended up frozen. And then the Sun King, powerless and upset, went to the glaistig for help. She gave him a locket that could only be wielded by a human—the locket she had gotten from Phoenix—and a prophecy that the human who wore the locket was destined to end the war, bringing in someone else as though he didn't think his son could handle it. And that had to have hurt Frost's ego.

She didn't believe the Sun Prince for a minute when he said he hadn't been able to tell her about this at the party because there were so many other faeries around. Frost had wanted her to butt out. He was upset that the Sun King had brought her in when he had Frost, and worried she would figure out that he had stolen the troves, getting him in trouble, opening the troves, and getting one of his parents hurt before he could figure out how to fix it. He probably thought that now that she had rejected his offer to work with him that she'd run straight to his father and tell him about the troves. And why shouldn't she? The Ice Queen was evil. Jade could tell that even if the Sun Prince couldn't.

But that brought up another problem: how exactly was she supposed go about telling the Sun King about his son, anyway? She could imagine, vividly, exactly how that conversation would go. After all, why would the Sun King—or anyone in the Forever Court, really—believe her, a stranger and a pixie, over the Sun Prince, particularly without proof? Frost could just move the troves before they had a chance to raid his room, and then she would look stupid in front of the whole Forever Court.

But Frost was right about one thing. The big question was: if Frost and Phoenix had stolen the Ice Queen's powers, how was she still able to freeze Phoenix and make winter encroach?

Jade racked her brains but could find no answers. It seemed impossible. Gods, she was so not good at this! What did she know about magic? She was just a girl! They needed someone more experienced, someone braver, someone cleverer. Someone like . . .

"Vira Wyvernsting!" Pip's faint voice echoed as though she were still a fair distance away.

Vira Wyvernsting. Of course. This was why they wanted Vira. Jade was no good at this kind of thing. Riddles, logic puzzles . . . she just didn't have the patience, particularly when the fate of a whole kingdom depended on her, the wrong girl, with time running out. All she'd managed to do so far was make an enemy of the Sun Prince and get the pixies who'd taken her under their wings into serious danger.

To make matters worse, it wasn't as though she could just abandon it all and go home—she was a pixie now, and she didn't even know *how* to go home. In fact, when it came down to it, she couldn't think of a single thing that was going right. This was really not how she had envisioned her first adventure.

The sun was setting, lighting up the frost on the leaves in shades of brilliant red and gold. And she only had one day left. Her nose tingled, and her eyes blurred.

She tore off her red cap and threw it on the ground. If this was adventure, Vira could keep it. Jade blinked, trying to keep the tears from flooding her eyes.

"Vira Wyvernsting, where are you?" Pip called, sounding closer this time.

Why couldn't Pip have figured it out before Jade put the locket on? Why couldn't the pixie have stopped her back then, when it was still her birthday, and she was still at home? Sure, Jade would have had a bad night, maybe even stormed off and cried a lot, but the faeries would be all right, and she would be with her family, and none of this mess would have happened. Now, even if she could get home, her family wouldn't recognize her. She was a pixie, and while it seemed great at first—flying was beyond compare—it also meant she had no home to return to, either in the Feywild or back in Oakspring.

What a mess she had gotten herself into. And it was all the locket's fault—the locket and that stupid prophecy. She took the locket—the worst birthday present ever—in her hands.

"Vira Wyvernsting? Is that you?" She saw Pip's shadow in the soft phosphorescence of the mushrooms on the dark trees.

"Hi, Pip," Jade said, thinking only about how she had to get rid of the locket. At least then she could go home again. She yanked downward, but only succeeded in cutting the chain into the back of her neck.

"It *is* you!" Pip said, crossing over to her. "Thank goodness! Where have you been? I've been looking for you all afternoon!"

"Help me get this off," Jade said, gritting her teeth against the pain and trying again. The chain dug into her palms like fire, and she bit back a scream.

"What? No!" Pip said, flying and tugging Jade's hands away from the chain.

Despair began to well in the girl's throat. She couldn't go home. She couldn't go back to the Forever Court. She couldn't even go back to the pixies to hide—not after what Naomi had said in front of them all. And now, she couldn't even go home. Not with the stupid locket keeping her a pixie.

145

"What are you doing!" Pip asked. "I thought you wanted to go find Aron after chores?"

"Oh, Pip," Jade said, sitting down on one of the phosphorescent mushrooms and burying her face in her hands. The soft fungus quivered and let out a sporey sneeze. "I don't think I can do this anymore."

"Yes you can!" Pip flew down to grab the red cap off the ground and then flew back up to sit down next to Jade. "You are destined to. You're Vira Wyvernsting, the girl out of the prophecy!"

"But that's just it—I'm not!" Jade cried, looking at Pip with tears glistening in her eyes. "I'm not my sister, I don't know what I'm doing, no one is helping me, and every time I try to do anything someone gets hurt."

"That's not true . . ." Pip started.

"Yes it *is*," Jade said. "Maybe my sister would know what to do, but I'm . . . I'm just doing this all *wrong.*"

Jade took a deep breath and let it out slowly, trying to control her sobs.

"All I want is to go home," Jade said, softer, her voice choked. "But I can't even do that. Not like this! I'm not even human anymore!"

"No, you're not human," said Pip. "You're a pixie. And being pixie is way better than being a human." Strangely, Jade was not comforted.

"But what am I going to do?" Jade said. "None of this

was supposed to happen. I can't go home. I can't go back to the pixies. I can't go to the Forever Court. I can't confront the Sun Prince. And I can't lie anymore. It's just going to hurt people. It's already hurt people."

"Stop talking about what you can't do, about what was supposed to happen. None of that matters," Pip said. "What matters is what did happen: you ended up with the locket, not your sister—"

"Because I stole it," Jade murmured, but Pip talked right over her.

"—Davin and the rest of us pixies are all right and we don't care who you are. And unless you intend on dying, you had better just do the best you can, because you're the only hope we have," Pip said.

What a horrifying thought—the whole Forever Court dependent on her.

"Besides," Pip said, "in case you hadn't noticed, *you* defeated those spiders, not your sister."

"Spiders are a lot different than the Ice Queen," Jade said "And when that elf came, I froze."

"No, Davin froze," Pip said with a smirk. "You somehow managed to escape that fate."

This only made Jade feel more distressed.

"But even if you didn't defeat the elf, you can't win every time," Pip added quickly. "And besides, I haven't seen your sister around here defeating any elves, let alone dragons!"

Jade half laughed, half sobbed. Her sister was safe back at home, enjoying her ranger training.

"And who knows?" the pixie continued. "Maybe they were mistaken. Or perhaps the prophecy was wrong! I always liked you better anyway, no matter what anyone else says. You can do this. You can figure it out. You're really clever! And besides, you have me!"

"Thanks, Pip," Jade said, sniffling.

"And after this is all over, I'll help you figure out how to turn back into a human and get you home. I promise," Pip said.

If I'm not an icicle, Jade thought to herself. It was kind of Pip to offer.

"So, are you ready to go back now . . . Vira Wyvernsting?" Pip said, holding out the red cap. Jade looked at the red cap and at Pip's expectant face, and made a decision. She might have been wrong to abandon the faeries, but she was not wrong about one thing.

"My name is not Vira Wyvernsting," Jade said, pushing the red cap away. If she was going to help the faeries, she was going to do it under her name, in her way. "Call me Jade. Jade Farstar."

Chapter Fifteen

Jade Farstar and Pip were still arguing about whether they should go talk to the Sun King, try to steal the troves back and give them to him, confront the Sun Prince, or just find Aron and tell him everything when they saw a flash of blue-white light.

"Shhh . . . stop." Jade held out an arm, stopping Pip midflight.

A crackling sound shook air, and frost swept across the forest from some distant point, coating everything in a thick rime of frost. Flowers turned brown, wilted, and died. Leaves curled, withered, and fell. The birds all went silent, and Jade shivered. It seemed as though all the warmth and happiness had been sucked out of the air at once. Her locket felt like winter itself against her skin. This had to be the work of the Ice Queen.

"Quick, let's hide," Jade said.

"Over here!" Pip said, pointing to a hollow tree. They both dived inside, then hovered, cocking their pointed ears.

For a moment, all was quiet.

Then they heard a murmuring of voices that gradually got louder, as though the people were getting closer. Suddenly, the voice—sharp and feminine—was clear as ice, echoing inside the hollow of the tree: "I don't care what Naomi said. I am running out of patience, and you are running out of time. You do not want to disappoint me again."

The leaves rustled and branches of the tree they hid in swayed and tangled as though the forest itself were whispering a response to the haunting voice. Pip and Jade looked at each other. "The Ice Queen," Pip mouthed. Jade nodded. It had to be—no one else could sound like that. But who was she talking to?

"No, a girl without a locket is useless," the Ice Queen snapped. "How hard could it be to get the locket when the whole Forever Court is celebrating its arrival?" The locket. They were after the locket. That must be what Naomi had come for!

"Don't underestimate him!" the Ice Queen said. "If you give him enough time, he *will* find a way to stop me."

"Vira Wyvernsting?" the voice laughed, a sound like glass breaking. Jade froze upon hearing the name on the Ice Queen's lips. "Kidnapping her was obviously pointless. Discard her, let the redcaps have her, do with her as you see fit. She is useless—just another nuisance of a human girl. There are countless ones just like her where she comes from. I need the one with the locket. Unless"–there was a thoughtful pause–"unless you used her as bait to catch the one with the locket. I'm sure her sister cares about what happens to her."

"That hag!" fumed Pip. "How dare she say those things about you!"

"About my sister," Jade said, her heart pounding against her ribs. "I'm not Vira, remember?"

"Oh, right," Pip said.

It sounded like Vira wasn't safe at home at all. She was in a terrible danger, and it was all Jade's fault. Jade strained her ears, trying to hear something, anything more about her sister, where they were keeping her, how she was doing, how they were planning on using her as bait.

"Watch your tongue," the Ice Queen said. "You should be honored that I am treating with you and not simply destroying you for your past betrayal."

Jade ground her teeth. She needed to know who the queen was speaking to. That was the key. They must be speaking very quietly, so as not to be overheard. She began to fly stealthily out of the hollow tree, but Pip grabbed her arm and pulled her back down, shaking her head.

"That's a risk I am prepared to take," the Ice Queen said dryly. Jade Farstar was going to have to take some risks too if she wanted to solve this.

"What are you doing?" Pip hissed.

"I need to find out who she is talking to!" Jade said, and she shook herself free of Pip's arms and left the tree. It had to be the Sun Prince—he was the only one who knew where the troves were and how to open them, aside from her. She knew she couldn't trust him! First he tried to get her to agree to do whatever he said, and now that he thought she was running to tell his daddy, he was negotiating with the Ice Queen!

The frost was thicker to the east—away from the castle. She began flying in that direction, careful to dart between the highest tree branches, neither straying too low nor out in the open.

"No. The deal is, I want the locket and my trove back . . . tonight," the Ice Queen said. "The glaistig's riddle says the girl with the locket will end the war on the third night—that's tomorrow—and I know exactly how I want the war to end. If you get me the locket and return my magic to me here by dawn, you will have what you desire."

The Ice Queen's voice was fading. Forgetting secrecy, Jade sped up, trying to reach the source of the sound as fast as she could, wanting to catch Frost red-handed. But the light was fading. Jade strained her ears, keeping her hand pressed to her locket, listening to see if there was anything more, but nothing came. Eventually, the birds went back to singing. They were too late.

"You were right! The prince *is* striking a deal to stop the war," Pip cried upon reaching her.

At the same time, Jade said, "My sister's in trouble!"

"We have to stop them," Jade said, a new firmness in her voice.

"How? We don't even know where the Ice Queen's trove is," said Pip.

"I do," said Jade quietly. "And I know how to get it. But we'll need help."

"You do?" Pip asked, looking astonished. "But...nobody even knows who stole it."

"The prince and I had a very interesting conversation when we went to help Davin," Jade said.

"The glaistig was right," Pip said. "She warned you not to trust him!" Jade and Pip looked at each other grimly.

"We have to . . ." Jade began.

"You have to what?" the Sun Prince's sharp voice broke in.

"Oh no," Pip said. Jade's heart leaped into her throat.

"We were just . . ." Jade began. How much had he heard?

"Wait—" the Sun Prince said, his eyes narrowing.

He swept out a hand, and before Jade knew what was happening, he had her clutched lightly in one hand. Her heart pounded faster than a hummingbird's. He'd caught her! What if he brought her to the Ice Queen right now? Or worse, what if he just killed her and took the locket to the

Ice Queen and her sister? There was no one was around to hear her, and it was not as though she could defend herself. He raised his other hand, and Jade squeezed her eyes shut. She didn't want to die this way! But he just stroked her tuft of blonde-jade hair.

"Blonde . . . Vira Wyvernsting is not blonde. Where is she?" the Sun Prince said. "What have you done with her?"

What was this, some kind of game? He knew very well where Vira Wyvernsting was! That was the kind of question Jade was supposed to ask! Or was he just playing with her, trying to figure out how much she'd heard?

Jade struggled as the Sun Prince's grip tightened uncomfortably around her ribs, and then, suddenly sick of being chased and caught and cornered, pushed around like a little girl with no respect or thought for her well-being or her needs, she bit his hand as hard as she could. A pixie's teeth are surprisingly sharp, and the prince cursed and dropped her as blood welled in the cut. She flew up, safely out of reach, and glared down at him.

"Tell me where she is, you fool of a pixie!" Frost said, taking another swipe at her. But this time, Jade was ready, and she darted out of the way, avoiding capture.

"I think we both know the answer to that," Jade said hotly. But he had misjudged her. She had figured him out.

"You don't know what you're messing with," Frost said quietly.

"And you don't know *who* you're messing with," Jade said. "Stay away from me and mine if you know what's good for you!"

"I was just about to say the same to you," Frost said, and she saw ice in his solid blue eyes. Before she could say another word, he spun on his heel and left, striding back to the castle, a cold breeze rising in his wake.

"I can't believe it," Pip said, staring after him, her eyes as big as twin moons. "You just told off the Sun Prince!"

"That's the least of what I mean to do," Jade said, thinking of her sister and her resolution to save the faeries of the Forever Court—even if it was from one of their own. There was only one thing she couldn't figure out. She was suddenly furious. She had been used.

"And the Sun Prince turned against his own father!" Pip said.

"I knew he would try to make a deal with her," Jade said. "I knew he couldn't be trusted. I just didn't know how bad it had gotten. To think, he's had my sister all this time!"

"I . . . I don't believe it," Pip said.

"Believe it," Jade said grimly. "Because it's up to us to stop him."

"Us?" Pip said. "We can't do anything—we're just pixies, and I hate to be the one to tell you, but no one listens to pixies."

"That's exactly why it has to be us. Who would believe

us?" Jade said. "It's our word against the Sun Prince's! And believe me, I have experience. When it's your word against the word of the golden child, you are always, always wrong. Even if the golden child is actually a spoiled, lying brat."

"But what can we do?" Pip said.

"We're going to give the faeries a reason to respect pixies," Jade said. "We're going to stop the Ice Queen—even if it means taking down the Sun Prince. We're going to steal the troves—before he has a chance to hand them over to the Ice Queen tonight."

Chapter Sixteen

Jade Farstar peeked around the corner. The hallway was dark, no one was in sight, and the two stone dragons sat silent and motionless on either side of the door to Frost's chambers. This late at night, no one should be about, save Frost. She flattened herself against the wall on the other side again and turned to her assembled crew, all astride ravens.

While faeries could fly, they could not carry as heavy a load as the ravens, and the birds were excellent for carrying the extra-large-sized devices she'd had the pixies make for this adventure. And besides, the mirrors looked rather heavy. It might even take all of them and their ravens to carry the troves out. But first things first: they had a mission to accomplish that night. She surveyed the pixies' faces.

Quinn looked reluctant, but his wings hummed with determination, and Pip looked intent. Pip had been against including Quinn initially, claiming very unpixielike displays of poor sportsmanship, but Jade eventually convinced her that they needed his skill with silence traps. She was glad she had managed to convince Pip of his usefulness. Quinn, at least, looked ready to go. Reeva looked resigned, but Davin looked nervous, and no wonder—he'd gotten the raw end in their last two adventures. Jade decided they could use a bit of a pep talk.

"All right, remember: we can do this," Jade began. "Sure, they're bigger and more powerful. But we're clever, and we're in our element. What do pixies do best?"

"Prank," said Quinn sarcastically, clearly in his element.

"Yes. Prank," Jade confirmed. "Think of this as one big, extended prank."

"It's all just a prank," Davin murmured to himself while shaking his head.

"It's a lot more than that," Reeva said, sighing. "It's treason."

"Mmmm, delicious treason!" Pip said. "Better than a hot sticky bun."

"It's not treason," Jade said. "It's the biggest service we can do for the Forever Court—protecting it against betrayal from the inside, where it would never see it coming. If we do this, we'll be heroes!"

"Heroes," Davin said nervously. "That sounds a lot better than traitors."

"I'm with you," Reeva said to Jade. "But you had better be right."

"Good," Jade said. That would have to do. "All right, Quinn? On the count of three."

"One."

The pixies tensed.

"Two."

Quinn lifted a glass ball filled with smoke.

"Three!"

Quinn expertly threw the glass ball against the nose of the first dragon, where it shattered with a puff of white smoke, and the pixie immediately threw a second glass ball on the nose of the other dragon. The two dragons opened their mouths to scream a warning, and Jade held her breath—but no sound came out. She peered closer. Their stony tongues were tied in an expert pixie knot. She waited a moment longer to see if they would leap off their posts, but they stayed statues, soundlessly wailing an alarm no one would hear.

She motioned for the faeries to get into position.

Buzzing up to the door, she tried to remember the exact order Frost had touched them in. He had traced his fingers over the carvings, and she flew in the same pattern his hand had followed, pressing in first a rose—it took both of her arms to his one slender finger—then . . . a star? No, a sun, and then the carving of a stag.

She held her breath, half expecting it not to work, for the dragons to start howling, for the guards to come—but then the door evaporated, just as it had before. Jade let out a giant sigh of relief.

Here goes nothing, she thought. Alone, she flew through the empty doorway and into the room. Immediately, her eyes flew to the bed—empty. Then she darted over to the wardrobe on the far side of the room and began tugging open the doors. It was hard because she was so small, but she managed to get them open, push the prince's garments aside, and pull out the false panel. Diving in, she began throwing silks aside—but the troves were gone! There must be some mistake. She threw more silks aside, but to no avail. There was only one answer: Frost had already turned the troves over to the Ice Queen. They were too late.

Just then a weary sigh made her snap around.

Frost stood in a darkened corner, watching her. His solid, sapphire blue eyes were hard as ice. He held his hands behind his back.

"It didn't have to be this way," Frost said, walking toward her. "We could have worked together."

"I would never work for you!" Jade said, but her mind raced. If he was already here, he might already have the troves ready for the Ice Queen. Maybe he was just waiting to add her—and the locket—to the package!

"I really didn't think you'd figure it out. I mean, you're a pixie," Frost said, shaking his head. "To think I gave you the keys to my own betrayal."

"Too bad," Jade taunted. How had he known she was going to break in that night, anyway? "Guess I'm smarter than you gave me credit for." Was there a leak among the pixies? Reeva, she thought. It had to be Reeva. Or Davin, whom Frost had saved. She wondered if even now, they were watching her, thinking she got her just desserts. If that were true, Pip was in trouble too. She felt a stab of guilt. Poor Pip. She hadn't signed up for any of this.

"There's just one thing I can't figure out," Frost said. "Why'd you come back?"

"Because all faeries deserve the—" Jade began, before she realized what the prince had actually said. "Wait. Why'd I do what?" She had a suspicion that something had gone horribly wrong.

"Did you forget the password?" Frost asked. "Were you hoping to find it somewhere in there? As though I'd be stupid enough to write it down."

"You think I stole the troves?" Jade exclaimed.

"And what did she offer you that we couldn't?" Frost demanded, his eyes intense, his face furious. "Did she tell you she'd take you home if you gave her the locket and trove? That she'd turn you back into a human? You selfish, stupid pixie. We could have helped you with all that. You have just doomed all the Forever Court."

"No . . . no, that's not what happened at all," Jade protested. This was all wrong! The prince thought *she* had stolen the trove? Well, granted, she was planning on stealing the trove, but she hadn't yet, and she certainly hadn't planned on giving it to the Ice Queen.

"I first suspected something was wrong right after you'd left here. I found Naomi missing from the library, poor Aron unconscious. Didn't want her to break your cover, did you? But did you really think that after hearing the Ice Queen talking to you in the forest, I wouldn't figure out what you were up to?" Frost said. "That I wouldn't be ready for you? You are the only one, aside from me, who knows where the troves are or how to open them."

Her own logic, thrown back at her. The implications hit her harder than a brick. Her wings almost stopped beating. It wasn't the Sun Prince. He wasn't the one she'd heard bargaining with the Ice Queen. And now he thought *she* was working with his mother. But if he wasn't the one in the forest, and she knew it wasn't her, then who was? Frost was right. She hadn't known what a mess she was getting herself into.

"No—" Jade started. But she remembered how firm she had felt in her conviction, and it did look really bad for him to have caught her breaking in. Frost crossed his arms. It had been someone else speaking to the Ice Queen in that forest, someone who knew where the troves were.

"I really thought you would have given the troves to my father, the way you were talking back there," the Sun

Prince said. "But you were just playing me too, weren't you?"

"No, you don't understand," Jade said. "I *was* going to give them to your fath–I mean . . . You were defending the Ice Queen so much, and you stole the troves, and I overheard someone telling the Ice Queen they'd bring her the winter trove and the locket tonight, and I thought she was talking to you. And no one would believe me if it was my word against you, so I had to stop you before–"

"You pixies are so glib with your lies," Frost said. He sighed. "I can't tell the difference between your lies and your truths. I am going to take you to my father."

"And tell him what?" Jade retorted. "That you stole his power and that of the Ice Queen, and that I was trying to steal it back?"

"And tell him about your conversation with the Ice Queen," the prince said. "That you lied about being Vira is proof enough of your character. And when Aron finally wakes up, I'm sure he'll be happy to tell us all exactly what happened with Naomi." Frost barked a laugh. "As if I needed proof. As you said, who would believe the word of a pixie against me?"

"But–" Jade started.

"No buts," the Sun Prince said. "This game is over. Now, just hand over the troves and we'll make this as painless as possible. At least until we figure out whose side you're really on."

But she was also right—the prince didn't know who he was dealing with either. "I'm so sorry about this, Your Highness," she said, and as she said it, she noticed his hand was held behind his back in the exact same way he had when he held the petal pollen. She was sorry now that she knew he was innocent. But that didn't change what she had to do. He was still standing in the way of her saving her sister and stopping the Ice Queen, no matter how good his intentions. Her sister needed her now. "The hydra has hatched!" she shouted.

"I thought you'd never say that!" called Quinn, grinning ear to ear. Swooping down from above, half hanging off of his giant raven, he let out a wild whoop and pulled open the release of the bag his raven held, releasing hundreds of glitterbombs. Frost looked up just in time to see the tiny pellets splash on his face, his shoulders, and all around him, filling the air with a storm of bright, blinding glitter.

"Give up now," Frost said. "There's still time for you to do the right thing!" And he raised the hand he had behind his back.

"Pip!" Jade called. "Hit his left hand!"

"Got it!" Pip called out, flying in on her own raven. With expert aim, she signaled to her raven to squeeze the life out of the giant waterskin it carried, just as the prince opened his hand. A heavy stream of water drenched the pollen, washing away its potency.

"Eeech!" Frost exclaimed, and Jade felt a wave of satisfaction. So even pampered elf princes weren't prim and proper all the time. And just on time, Davin swooped in, followed by Reeva, whose bird carried the heaviest load of all.

"I'm sorry, Your Highness!" Davin said.

"Is that you, Davin?" the prince said, still blinded by the glitter and waving his wet and sparkling hands. "But I saved you!"

"It's for your own good," Davin answered. He dropped his trick rope around the prince's ankles. The rope snaked up Frost's legs, weaving around, and the prince began hopping blindly, trying to shake it off.

"You don't know what you're doing!" Frost said. "You have to—"

"For the pixies!" Reeva cried, and her raven swooped low, carrying a monster load—a melon-sized ball woven from three hundred blades of grass and filled to bursting with their stickiest stickyball glue.

"Reeva?" Frost said in disbelief. "I thought you had more sense than this!"

"Whatever do you mean, Your Highness?" Reeva answered. "I am just a pixie! Your words, I'll have you remember!"

"That's not what I meant—" Frost started.

And she dropped that mother of all stickyballs right at his feet. Frost blinked his eyes clear of the glitter just in time to get his hands out in front of him as Davin pulled the trick rope tight around his legs. Frost fell to the ground, placing his feet, his knees, and his hands firmly in the glue that held him glittering, fuming in place.

"Tell it to your father," Jade said.

"You should have listened to us!" Pip said as she banked for Jade's position. Jade leaped astride Pip's raven, right behind the pixie. "Now you'll just get to hear about the adventure after it's done!"

The pixies circled the room and the glued, glittered, and amazed prince once, then streamed out the door.

"No!" Frost called out. "You don't understand. That's why Phoenix and I stole the troves—to stop the war. If my father gets his trove—the war will continue, worse than ever. And someone might get hurt!"

"In case you hadn't noticed," Jade said, "people have already gotten hurt!"

"But—" the prince started.

"Have you forgotten Phoenix already?" Jade asked. "She said she believed in second chances. She didn't want you to run away when she was frozen! She knew she might fail when she confronted the Ice Queen, and she wanted to give you a chance to try again if she did."

"But we still don't know how the Ice Queen froze her without her powers," Frost said. "And don't you see? She needs the locket to activate the trove. If you go to her, you'll be playing right into her hands."

"Don't worry about us, prince!" Pip said.

"Yeah," Jade said. "All we have to do is catch the thief before he gets the trove to the Ice Queen!"

"Yeah!" Pip said. Then their time was up, and the dragons started screaming in earnest. Kicking her heels, Pip wheeled the raven away after the other faeries.

"Who are you, anyway?" Frost called after her.

"I'm Jade!" she shouted over her shoulder. "Jade Farstar. And I will find the trove and the thief, rescue my sister, and stop the Ice Queen. You wait and see!"

Chapter Seventeen

The faeries met back at the edge of the pixie glen, their ravens clacking their beaks with excitement. The night was still young, and Jade Farstar estimated they had eight hours before the sun started to break over the horizon. Eight hours to rescue her sister, retrieve the troves, and defeat the Ice Queen. Eight hours until the prophecy said she would end the war—one way or another.

"Thank you," Reeva said. "I haven't had fun like that in years. It was good to show everyone what it means to be a pixie."

"Are you sure you'll be all right?" Jade asked.

"We'll be fine," Reeva answered. "Davin, Quinn, and I will lie low for a couple days, but I doubt the Sun Prince will confess to being bedazzled by pixies. What self-respecting elf would?"

"We'll see you when we have answers," Jade said, waving as she and Pip settled their raven down in the boughs of an ancient, gnarled tree with silver-leafed branches that fell around it like a waterfall. The wind made a sighing sound as it rustled through the long, sweeping branches.

Someone had made a deal with the Ice Queen—and it wasn't Frost. Admittedly, that set Jade back a fair amount. She had really thought he was the one. If he wasn't, who could it possibly be? It had to be someone who knew where the troves were. As far as she knew, that list extended to Frost and herself. Clearly, someone else had figured it out.

It couldn't be the Ice Queen—she wanted someone to steal the trove for her. The idea of it being the Sun King was as farfetched as wondering if she herself were the culprit. Phoenix was frozen in ice, so she wasn't up to stealing much of anything. And if Frost had made the deal, he was very convincing in his heroic attempts to subdue her as the thief. Who else could it be?

"Are we really going after the thief?" Pip asked, interrupting her train of thought. "Once we figure out who he is, I mean?"

"He has my sister and the troves," Jade said simply. "We have to stop him."

"But you heard the Ice Queen—it's a trap!" Pip said. "He's just using your sister to get to you—and the locket."

"I know," Jade said. "But that doesn't mean my sister doesn't still need me. Besides, the Ice Queen is going to be after me anyway. I don't want to just wait for her to catch up with me. I want to do something!"

"I don't suppose we can go talk to the Sun King . . ." Pip said.

"You know he doesn't have any power," Jade said. "Besides, he seemed to expect *me* to save *him*. And it ends tonight." The prophecy said so.

"Or Aron," Pip pressed.

"He's still unconscious, and likely guarded," Jade said. "With my sister's life on the line, I can't just wait for him to wake up!" The Sun King trusted Jade. She couldn't let him down now. "Besides, it's going to take forever for them to sort through what's going on when they find the prince all trussed up in his room, and I have a feeling that if we're there, we'll never get to my sister in time."

Think, think! Was there anything else that the Sun King had said, aside from his plea and offer of Aron's help, anything else about the prophecy? What else had happened that night? Jade thought back to that evening, stepping through her conversation with the king, then the prince, and then . . . She gasped. That was it.

The king's prophecy wasn't the only one she'd heard that night. There was a second prophecy, this one just for her. And it had come true too.

"So what are we going to do?" Pip said.

"That night I talked to the glaistig, and she also told

me a prophecy," Jade said. "When Frost has lost what he once took, and you would do what he forsook . . ." Jade said, "find me."

"Oh no," Pip said.

"We have to visit the glaistig," Jade said.

"No! Jade, that is the *worst* idea," Pip said.

"Don't you see? Her prophecy came true!" Jade said. "Frost stole the troves, and then he lost them. Now, I want to do what he didn't and confront the Ice Queen!"

"Have you forgotten that she's also the one whose 'prophecies' said that you're the wrong girl?" Pip said. Jade winced. Like she could forget. "She doesn't make prophecies, that's just what everyone calls them. She collects and sells secrets!"

"But that's exactly what we're after!" Jade said. "Secrets. Like who the thief is and where he's keeping my sister, how the Ice Queen was able to freeze Phoenix and make winter encroach without her powers, and how to defeat the Ice Queen. We're running out of time. Do you have a better idea?"

"You're new to the Feywild, so you may not know this," Pip said. "But glaistigs eat people."

Jade tried to wrap her mind around that.

"Like, chew and swallow their flesh?" Jade said. Now she understood Pip's reaction to the glaistig. She was glad she hadn't known that when the glaistig had approached her outside the Forever Court! She would have been even more terrified.

"More like, break their bones and drink their blood," Pip said. "Glaistigs are dark, dangerous faeries."

"How do you know so much about them, then, if you avoid them so much?" Jade asked.

"My grandpop visited one once. She has to be the same one you're talking about, the only one that dares visit the fringes of the Forever Court," Pip said. "She lives in the River of Secrets."

Jade shook her head to clear the image of the glaistig's sharp, needlelike teeth from her head. "What happened to your grandpop?"

"He had the bright idea of trying to steal a secret from the glaistig," Pip said. "He survived, but barely. And the brownies had to make him a new set of wings afterward."

Jade's wings shivered involuntarily. She couldn't even imagine how much that would hurt—but also, how long it must have taken him, at only a few inches high, to walk back on foot. She made a note not to steal from the glaistig.

"Jade Farstar, I'm telling you, you really don't want to get involved with glaistigs," Pip said. "They're dangerous, bad creatures."

"More dangerous than the Ice Queen?" Jade said. "Look, if you want to go home, I understand. But my sister and the whole Forever Court are depending on me. I'm not going to let them down."

Pip's wings drooped, but she didn't turn the raven around.

"East it is, then," Pip said, sighing. "Closer to the Ice Queen, and the ice, and the snow."

"Thanks, Pip," Jade Farstar said, hugging her. Pip looked back at her and gave her a small, lopsided smile.

"But you have to promise me we won't stay long, all right?" Pip said. "Winter does not do good things to summer faeries. After a couple days, I'd be as frozen as Phoenix."

"Don't worry," Jade said. "This shouldn't take long." Not more than eight hours, anyway, one way or another.

Flying over the Feywild was an amazing sight. After leaving the pixie glen, they flew over the Eternal Woods, the dark forest where they had overheard the Ice Queen. Eventually, the woods thinned, and they passed a citadel that glittered as though it were made of diamonds. "Spun sugar, actually," Pip had corrected. Home to the banshraes, it was ironically made of all the most delicious foods in the world that they could no longer eat. Then they passed over a lake whose depths glimmered with castles made of sand, past a forest of ancient trees that almost seemed to move beneath them, and into a forest of bone white trees whose tangled reaches were painted red, and in which rusting old scythes split the ground like crumbling teeth. The redcaps' home. Jade Farstar began to wish that she hadn't gotten rid of her red cap. She could be forthcoming about who she was without having to throw caution to the winds, couldn't she? But she had never been good about doing things halfway.

At last they approached a river so wide the far bank was obscured in the mists. The near bank was carpeted in flowers—bluebells, violets, and jasmine, with a scattering of the electric blue mushrooms she had grown used to—before it gave way to a blanket of moss-covered stones. A wooden bridge, painted gold and red and lined with lanterns, spanned the river. As she got closer she saw that the river's waters were a deep sapphire, almost black and thick with jewel-like fish, some as small as she was, and some as big as a dog. A worn wooden sign above the river was painted, "Way Home."

The words put a thrill through her. Was it true? Could this prove the way home? Jade glanced over at Pip, wondering if the pixie saw the same words, or if it read differently to her, as was possible in a land of magic.

Then the raven balked and would go no farther, squawking and shaking its head whenever they tried to drive it onward, ruffling its feathers unhappily. So Pip had the raven set down. After feeding it a piece of raw apple from her knapsack, Jade and Pip flew cautiously on alone to the river.

It felt good to stretch her own wings, but she couldn't help but notice that some of what she'd previously thought were moss-covered stones along the riverbank were actually sun-bleached helms, swords, and shields. A silver horseshoe on a chain lay discarded among the rubble amid a scattering of silver coins whose make she did not know. A muddy ribbon with one end trapped under an old shoe someone no longer needed fluttered in the breeze. And strange, white, curved shapes poked out of the bank like the teeth of a comb. She tried not to think about what those were.

Pip was shivering beside her. "I don't like this place at all," Pip said, pulling at her arm. "Come on, let's go home. We can find your answers elsewhere."

"Where else? We don't have long left! And the prophecy said to come here," Jade said. Home—as though she had one to return to. That's why she was here. "We are not leaving until we get some answers." She was scared too. But what choice did she have?

"Ahhhh," came a throaty, raspy sigh. The smell of rotting fish washed over Jade in a wave, and she had to suppress a coughing fit. Pip gagged.

The water bubbled and spit as though it were boiling, and a head of long, white hair split the surface, followed by a familiar face. The glaistig's lips were eerily bright red—as though they had been painted—with her sharp white smile in stark contrast. She wore the same dress with the sky blue ruffles and smell of wet goat.

The glaistig rose out of the water as though pulled from some invisible force from above, the water spilling off her like she were a fountain, until she was only thigh deep in the river. After stretching her spine and fingers with a series of *pops*, she glided to the shore with barely a wave, parting the water as easily as a shark.

"I knew you would come to me," the glaistig said, her red tongue flicking over her needlelike teeth. "Hungry minds always find me eventually."

"This was a bad idea," Pip whispered. "I want to go."

Privately, Jade agreed with her, but she had to have answers. She stood her ground as the glaistig closed the distance between them, until the glaistig was so close that Jade could see the red circles around the irises of her eyes.

"That's far enough," Jade said, wondering what she would do if the glaistig ignored her. The glaistig paused, looking surprised, and then threw back her head and laughed. Pip took an involuntary, fluttery step backward.

"You may have gotten smaller, but you have grown bold," the glaistig said. "It's been a long time since someone dared tell me what to do in my own home."

"I don't have a lot to lose," Jade said.

"So you don't indeed. Let's hope you have enough to give to make it worth my while," the glaistig said. "Welcome to my home, Jade and Pip of the pixies. I am Ciara, Lady of the River of Secrets, and you have need of me."

"I don't have time for games," Jade said.

"Then why are you here?" Ciara said. "For games are what we do in the Feywild."

"I need your help," Jade said. "My sister is in trouble." She hadn't intended to start with that. Pip looked at her urgently. "And the Forever Court. Someone stole the troves—again, I mean—and we need to know who it is this time because whoever it is, they made a deal with the Ice Queen. And also, we need to know how she is still using winter magic without her trove, because somehow we have to stop her from taking over. And—"

"And?" Ciara said.

"And I need to know how to get this locket off," Jade said, flashing a guilty look at Pip. "So I can turn back into a human and go home."

"Well. Is that all?" Ciara said. "It would take you . . . let's see"—the glaistig's eyes looked up as she did some mental calculations—"one hundred and one years to earn all those answers."

"But I don't have a hundred years!" Jade said.

"Imagine that," Ciara said. "There's another option, though it's a little more risky. Surely too risky for a girl such as yourself with dreams of going home some day . . ."

"I don't like where this is heading," Pip said.

"Quiet, Pip," Jade said. "What is it?"

"Secrets are my trade, my life, my blood," Ciara said. "Give me a secret I do not know, and I will give you a secret worth the same amount. Minus the cost of the exchange, of course."

"How do I know how much a secret is worth?" Jade asked.

"Why that's simple," Ciara said. "Tell me your secret, and I'll tell you what it's worth."

"That hardly seems fair," Jade said.

"You could always go back home empty-handed," Ciara said, shrugging. "Oh, that's right, you don't have a home."

"You are not a very nice person," Jade said, feeling manipulated, but feeling like she had little choice in the matter. She was already racking her brains for a secret the glaistig might be interested in.

"My dear, I'm not a person at all," said Ciara. "I'm a glaistig, and this is what I do—what I live for. It's not a charity."

"Don't do it," Pip said. "What guarantees do you have that she'll keep her word? Or that she won't just claim to already know every secret?"

"It's all right, Pip," Jade said. "Why would she play this game if she didn't?"

"Because she's evil," Pip said. "And she likes to play with her food before it dies."

"I am bound by my word," Ciara said, placing a hand on her heart.

"See?" Jade said, but Pip looked unconvinced.

"No!" said Pip. "All right. Just . . . let's get out of here quickly."

Jade couldn't agree more. What did she know worth knowing? What was a secret? She doubted the glaistig cared to hear about her personal secrets. She could only think of one secret worth anything to someone in the Feywild. She felt a bit of guilt about selling it, as it wasn't really her secret, but she was doing it for the faeries' own good. And she couldn't see any other options.

"I know who first stole the Sun King and Ice Queen's troves," Jade said. The Sun Prince would just have to change the location—and the locks. Too many people knew about it already, anyway. But the glaistig just shook her head.

"I've been trading in that secret for some time now," Ciara said. "Good people are so very bad at keeping secrets. Tell me you have something better."

"I do, I do!" she said as the glaistig wet her teeth. Jade did not want to know what would happen if she failed to play the game to the glaistig's satisfaction. Now what did she have? She thought back on all the events of the past few days.

Frost had said that to enter the Ice Queen's trove, it required both her locket and the correct password—and he hadn't told her that until she had him trussed and glued on the floor of his own chambers. That had to be valuable—the prince seemed to think it was, anyway.

"What are you thinking about?" Ciara said, flaring her nostrils.

And in addition, it was something few people knew—not even the Ice Queen knew the password to open her trove. It was a true secret, a dark secret, and a dangerous secret. It was one that once loose, made it even more dangerous for the Summer Kingdom if the trove got into the Ice Queen's hands. But, Jade figured, if the Ice Queen got her trove, Jade had already lost.

"Yes, yes this one," Ciara said. "It smells delectable . . ."

If this worked, she was really going to owe Frost an apology.

"Tell it to me, child," Ciara said.

She took a deep breath and hoped she wasn't putting the Forever Court in more danger than it was in already.

"I've been in the Ice Queen's trove," Jade said.

"Yes," Ciara said. "And . . . ?"

"And I know how to open it," Jade finished, hoping she wasn't making the biggest—and last—mistake of her life.

"Ah," Ciara sighed. "Now that, I can use."

"So if I tell you this," Jade said, "you'll tell me what I want to—"

The glaistig held up a finger. "Ah-ah, not yet." Ciara made a gesture, and what Jade thought was just a pile of rocks cleared, revealing a toothy-mouthed bowl. Waving her fingers over the pool, Ciara dragged her sharp, curving nails through the surface of the water, tracing shapes and leaving lines of light. Then, without looking at Jade, she curled an imperious finger. "Whisper it to the water," she murmured.

Jade flew closer and brought her lips to the water. The mists parted, and she could hear voices murmuring at her in the water. If she strained, she thought she might be able to even make out what they were saying.

"Quickly now, girl," Ciara said. "The magic is short-lived. You must give it the whole secret before it ends."

Jade began to whisper about the Ice Queen's trove, the way it looked, Frost's words, the way her locket had glowed, and the way the surface of the mirror had glowed and crawled like silver beetles. As she watched, murmuring everything she could remember, the water began to glow from within.

"More, give it more detail," Ciara whispered. "Make it real."

As Jade started to describe the way it felt when the cold metal of the mirror had enveloped her fingers, she felt the magic take hold. The water grew brighter and started to bubble, and the mist rose like a snake and she could feel herself breathing it in. Words came tumbling out faster than she could think, describing the exact temperature of the mirror, the exact shape of the shadows, the exact hue of the frame.

Then she felt something cold wriggling on her tongue. Revolted, she opened her mouth, and to her surprise, a jewel-like fish with cold silver scales and a scrolling pattern in black etched on its fins, a fish far larger than her mouth should hold, poured out and into the pool. It swam in tight circles in the pool, as though fighting confinement. She looked into its glassy black eyes and saw winter. Shuddering, she looked away.

So that's what Ciara meant by make it real, to give all of the details of the Ice Queen's trove. Jade tried to think about what she'd spoken to the water, but found her mind slipping as soon as she tried to put her finger on it.

"Thank you," Ciara said, admiring the fish. "This will do nicely."

Jade tried again. She had been talking with Frost inside his chambers, seen the Ice Queen's trove, and . . . and nothing.

"It's gone!" Jade said. "I can't remember it. I can't remember anymore . . ."

"I told you she couldn't be trusted!" said Pip.

"Yes. Oh, didn't I explain?" Ciara said. "That's how it works. You have a secret, and you give it to me."

"No, you didn't explain!" Jade said, flushing with the embarrassment of having been tricked—tricked when Pip was right there warning her it would happen! What if she needed that secret?

"Well, if you want it back," Ciara said, "I'm sure we could come to an arrangement."

"You'd better just give it back, you evil—" Pip began.

Jade gritted her teeth. "No, Pip. I've come this far," she said. What did it matter, really, that she no longer knew how to open the Ice Queen's trove? That was safer, actually, wasn't it? In case she got captured. "Now, it's my turn. Will you forget your secrets as well?"

"Of course not, my dear pixie. What kind of a merchant would do that?" Ciara smiled. "Now, this is a nice fish. I don't have many silver fish of this size. It'd say it is worth a full answer to one of your questions."

"Just one!" Jade said.

"I know. Life is full of tough choices, friend pixie," Ciara said. "Which one do you want the most?"

But Jade just had too many questions—her mind buzzed with them—and she needed answers to all of them. Where was Vira and how could she help her? How could she get the locket off so she could turn back into a human and go home? Who had stolen the troves from the prince's wardrobe? How was the Ice Queen still accessing her powers without her trove? And how could Jade defeat the queen?

"I really don't have all day," Ciara said as she scooped the silver fish out of the pool with both of her clawed hands. It wriggled and twisted, trying to get free, gasping as it suffocated.

"I'm thinking!" Jade snapped. Only one question. She tried to think of some way she could ask a clever question that would give her more than one answer.

"Come on," said Pip. "Just ask who the thief is and let's go home!"

"Is that your question?" Ciara asked Jade pointedly. "Remember, you can ask anything."

The glaistig took the fish over to the River of Secrets and dropped it in with a splash, where it was quickly lost in the thick, teeming schools of jewel-like fish, each one a secret, Jade realized. She wondered what the black one with the golden fins was, or the peach-colored one with the black fins and eyes like a crystal. That last one seemed to be watching her intently.

"Its value is decreasing," Ciara said.

"Just give me a moment," Jade said. Her sister? The Forever Court? Or how to get home?

But she knew she didn't need more time to think about it. As much as she wanted to go home and as much as she knew she needed to help save the Forever Court,

185

she loved her sister—more than the Feywild, more than this crazy adventure. Her sister had always been there for her, and now, Vira was at risk only because of Jade's actions. Besides, her sister was really smart. She was sure Vira could help her solve the mystery if only Jade could find her.

"I know my question," Jade said finally. "How do I save my sister?"

"That question is too big and too complicated," Ciara said. "You would need to divulge many more secrets for that particular school of fish. Try again."

"All right," Jade said. "Who is holding my sister captive?"

"Finally!" Pip said.

"Now that's something I can work with. But are you sure?" Ciara said, raising an eyebrow. "You would choose that question over ever going home and seeing your family again, over your responsibilities to the Forever Court, the Sun King, the Sun Prince, Pip, and all the summer faeries depending on you?"

"Yes," Jade said firmly, her stomach twisting as she said it. She glanced guiltily at Pip, but the pixie nodded at her reassuringly. It sounded awful when it was put it that way. But hadn't the Ice Queen made a deal with the person holding Vira captive? Perhaps Jade wasn't betraying the Forever Court after all. While the person who stole the troves might or might not be the person who held Vira captive, that person was the only one who had a deal with the Ice Queen—so the kidnapper was likely to end up with the troves. Suddenly, Jade felt quite clever. Even Vira would have had a hard time coming up with that one.

"Very well," Ciara said. "That secret is a bigger than yours, but I like you, so I'll make an exception." She walked over to the River of Secrets, and after watching the dark waters for a moment, darted her hand in. It came out with a snow white fish with purple fins, much like the other fish—only this one had no mouth. Pressing a clawed finger into the fish—just hard enough to draw a drop of blood—she placed her finger in the pool and quickly traced a pattern over the water, leaving glowing lines shimmering on the surface.

When she was done, a purple mist steamed up from the pool.

"Breathe it in!" Ciara commanded. "Quickly now, before it fades!"

Jade leaned over the pool and took a tentative sniff of the purple mist—it smelled vaguely of ashes. This was what she had come for, she told herself. This was what she had sacrificed for. No fear now. And she inhaled the purple mist. The mist flooded her senses in seconds, overwhelming her so that she barely noticed the world around her. It smelled like ashes, earthworms, and sugar.

"What has no mouth but loves to sing?" she heard herself saying in a hollow voice. "Who has the trust of the Sun King?"

She and Pip looked at each other.

"We have to get back," Jade said. "Now."

Chapter Eighteen

It took them an endless-seeming hour to get back to the Forever Court, but once they were there, Aron's chambers were easy to find, being, like all banshrae abodes, made primarily out of sweets. Gingerbread walls, chocolate flooring, hard-candy paintings, butter pillows on a puff-pastry couch, and a gingerbread desk on which there was a gingerbread chest. The window, made of spun sugar, was hanging open, allowing for a light breeze to pass through.

"Oh no," Pip said after glancing inside. "The room's empty! What if we're too late? What if he's already taken the troves to the Ice Queen?"

"Then we can still save my sister," Jade said. As soon as she flew into the room, however, her locket started glowing like a falling star. Pip giggled.

"You look like a shimmerling!" Pip said.

"I don't know why it's doing this," Jade said, annoyed. "The last time it did this was when I was in the prince's chambers."

Looking around, Jade was struck by how incredibly odd it was that banshraes, whose mouths had been stolen by the Ice Queen and so could not eat or drink, would surround themselves with all the best foods that the kitchens of the Feywild had to offer. To make matters stranger, inside Aron's chambers were all manner of wind instruments. Flutes, recorders, and panpipes lined the walls, all making an odd fluty sound when the breeze blew across them.

No wonder the banshraes were bitter, if they surrounded themselves with signs of their loss all the time! But that just made it stranger. Why would Aron, who had lost his mouth to the Ice Queen, serve her?

"Oh gods," Pip whispered. "Look up."

Jade looked up and gasped. Hanging in an elaborate, human-sized birdcage crafted of gold filigree, was her sister, asleep, limbs poking through the bars and looking somewhat the worse for wear. It surprised her how large Vira was compared to her. She wondered if her sister would even recognize her.

Vira was still dressed in her old ranger clothes, but those clothes had been worn and tattered, and were caked in mud. Her shiny, sleek black hair, which Jade had always envied, was now a tangled nest, and there was a white streak running through it that hadn't been there before. Her cheeks looked pale and drawn, and her lips were cracked and chapped as though she had not eaten, drunk, or slept well in a long time.

She wondered how long her sister had been in that cage. She looked like she'd been driven across half of the Feywild before she was imprisoned. Had it all been terrible? Jade felt a stab of guilt, but quickly swallowed it. Guilt was not productive. Getting her sister out of that cage, now that would be productive. But how to do it?

"How did no one see this?" Jade asked. Surely Aron had visitors from time to time.

"Oh that's easy," Pip said. "No one ever looks up unless they're a flyer. Walkers are such linear thinkers."

The cage was a fair distance off the ground, and it had a lock on it about the size of a human hand.

"Hold on just a minute," Pip said, reaching into her bag and pulling out what looked like human-sized lock-picks from her tiny, magic bag. "Aha!" Pip lifted them up triumphantly.

"Great!" Jade said. "Quickly now. I'll wake her up while you pick the lock."

"Got it!" Pip cried before launching herself, picks and all, at the lock. She attacked the lock with a ferocity only a pixie could show in such a delicate, skill-based maneuver. Jade shook head, smiling despite herself. Then she flew up to hover by her sister's ear.

Looking down at Vira, though, Jade lost her smile.

It was all wrong—it wasn't supposed to be this way. Jade should be the one in the cage. Vira had been the one in the prophecy. She was supposed to be the one who got the locket, and who worked with the Sun Prince to defeat the Ice Queen. Instead, she looked like she'd been used as a sled down the meanest, iciest slopes in the Feywild.

It's not my fault, Jade told herself. How was she to know that by taking the locket, her sister would end up kidnapped? She had thought Vira wouldn't get to visit the Feywild at all. That was *her* idea of revenge. And while that wasn't particularly nice of her, it also didn't stick her sister, beat up, in a cage.

Jade bit her lip but swallowed her guilt. Hovering over Vira's ear, she tugged on the lobe twice.

"Vira," she whispered. "Wake up."

"Who?" Vira said, her eyes snapping open.

"It's me!" Jade whispered. "Jade!"

"Jade?" Vira said.

"Yep!" Jade said, flying backward a bit and twirling so that Vira could get a good look. "It's me!"

"Oh no," Vira said. "They got you too. You ... you're a pixie! I thought I'd convinced them to leave you alone that day, but I must have done something wrong, something to pique their interest in you."

"Wait ..." Jade said. "So you weren't really upset with me?"

"Well, a little. You weren't taking the hint," Vira said, smiling wanly. "Oh, Jade. I'm so sorry. I knew I was in trouble by that point, but I'd hoped to keep you out of it. And here I was feeling bad for myself. Tell me"—she looked Jade in the eyes, as though she could read the answer there—"who did this to you?"

Jade had to stop herself from laughing because, she reminded herself, it was very serious to Vira. It wasn't Vira's fault she was behind the curve.

"No one did it to me," Jade said. "It's the locket—the one the faeries left for . . . me. And it's not that bad. Being a pixie is actually fun. You would love flying."

"So that's what the elves kept asking about," Vira said. "So who wrapped that trap around your neck?"

"It's not a trap," Jade said, vaguely annoyed. "It's a locket. And with it, I've had the most amazing adventures. Even you wouldn't believe some of them!"

"I don't believe what I'm hearing," Vira said.

"But we don't have time for this," Jade said. "I'm so glad I've found you. The Winter and Summer Kingdoms are at war, and Fro—I mean, someone—stole the Ice Queen's and Sun King's magic to try to stop it. But the Ice Queen somehow still has magic and froze her daughter and is bent on freezing all the Feywild. Then, in the forest, I heard her make a deal to get her trove—that's what contains all her magic—the locket, and me all delivered to her, which she thinks will win her the war because according to the prophecy, I . . . I mean, they expect that I will end the war by dawn. And I . . . I want to make sure we end it right."

She hoped she wasn't going too fast for Vira. She wasn't sure how much her sister knew already, but they really had to get moving. Her sister was just going to have to trust her.

"What are you talking about?" Vira said. "We need to get out of here. We need to get home! I'm not fighting the Ice Queen—the Ice Queen is who did all this to me. Don't you think I would have stopped her if I could?"

"Um, Jade Farstar? Vira Wyvernsting?" Pip said. "Cage is open."

"But . . . we have to!" Jade said, working with Pip to swing the cage door wide. It took both of them, one at the top and one at the bottom, to hold the heavy door open. "It's my fault they're in this mess. See, the locket really was for you. You were right. But I took it instead, and now the Forever Court might be doomed. But with both of us, they might be able to figure out how to make it work, anyway."

"Jade, they're manipulating you!" Vira said, scrambling out of the birdcage. She hung by her hands for a moment on the rim of the cage, dropped like a cat into a crouch, and rose to her truly—at this point—dominating height. Jade was very glad at that moment that she could fly, and she "stood" body to nose with her older sister. "Just like the winter faeries did to me, telling me what an honor it was to

194

be chosen by the elves to join their ranks as a human—when it turned out they just wanted to kidnap me."

"Can we do this later?" Pip said, looking nervously in the direction of the door. "Once we're out of here?"

"Quiet, Pip," Jade said. "That's awful, but I don't see what it has to do with me."

"You put on the locket instead of me because you found the locket first," Vira said. "You don't owe the faeries anything. This isn't your fault. You're a kid—your job is to be a good kid. Do you want to make our mother cry when you never come home?"

"Now who's being manipulative?" Jade said, but her thoughts went to Phoenix, caught in ice forever. Did her father cry when she never came home?

"Jade Farstar!" Pip said.

"Quiet!" Jade and Vira both snapped at the same time.

"Look, I know you don't want to believe it—your friends are so pretty, and shiny, and new—but they're using you," Vira said. "Stop and think about it. Are you willing to die for this? Would you be happy if these were the last days of your life? Not growing up, never playing in the woods again, never eating Mom's home-baked cookies—ever again?"

Home. It seemed like it had been forever since Jade had woken up on her birthday at home. The birthday crown. The smell of warm baked bread. The sheet over her lower bunk. It was a low blow. This wasn't about what she wanted or didn't want, though, and this wasn't about the faeries or her mother. This was about Jade doing what was right.

"If you don't want to come, you don't have to," Jade said. "But I'm going to go stop the Ice Queen, and I had *thought* that you could help."

"No, Jade . . ." Vira started.

"This isn't about you or Mom. This isn't about whether I want to go home or not. This is about finishing what I started. I took that locket even though I knew it was meant for you because I wanted an adventure. Well, I got one. And now I mean to make sure the good faeries win. Besides, they're my friends. I can't just leave them to die."

Suddenly, she became aware that both Pip and Vira were staring behind her, fear coloring their faces.

Clap. Clap. Clap. Clap.

Jade turned around to see Aron standing in the doorway clapping slowly and staring straight at her.

Chapter Nineteen

Very nice, Aron said directly into her mind. *Very . . . moving,* he continued. The banshrae sounded smooth and sweet as honey. Jade bet he would have had a marvelous singing voice. *Now that we are all here, let's get started, shall we?* And with a wave of his hand, the window and doors slammed and locked shut.

Vira screamed, and Pip immediately zipped to the window and tried to force it open. Aron just watched them, somehow seeming to smile without a mouth.

"Traitor!" Jade said. "You are the one who made the deal with the Ice Queen in the forest, aren't you?"

Very good, Aron said. *Did you come up with that all on your own? Or did you have help. From a lady in a river perhaps? Who visited you your first night at the Forever Court?*

"How did you know about that?" Jade said, starting to feel nervous. And how much did he know? A sinking feeling rose in her gut as the pieces started to come together.

"Yes now, 'Jade Farstar,' " Vira said. "We are about to

be killed because you won't give up on your fantasies of being a hero, because you were manipulated by a bunch of overgrown mosquitoes with a shiny necklace you could buy for two coppers at the local market!"

"Hey now!" Pip said. "You take that back! This overgrown mosquito freed your oversized butt!"

Thank you for bringing me the locket, Aron said, continuing to ignore everyone but Jade.

"Stay out of this!" Vira said.

"No, you stay out of this," Pip said. And she drew something out of her pocket Jade did not expect—a glass ball filled with smoke.

"Did Quinn—" Jade Farstar began.

"It's my last one," Pip said, grinning, and then threw the glass ball. It hit Vira in the middle of the forehead.

"What—" Vira began, and then her mouth moved, but no sound issued. Her tongue was tied in Quinn's trademark pixie knot. Vira looked furious.

"Much better," Pip sighed, and turned her attention back to Aron. Vira railed silently in the background.

And for the password to opening the Ice Queen's trove, Aron continued. *It will prove most helpful in my bargaining with her.*

"But I only told that to—" Jade started.

"The glaistig," Pip said darkly.

Foolish human. Did you think you were the only one to consult her? Aron said. He walked over to his flutes. Jade rotated in midair to watch him. He ran a contemplative hand over the assembled instruments. *Who exactly did you think gave Ciara the secret that led you here? Did you think it was an accident that you got that information? Or, better yet, did you think it was your skill?*

Jade hadn't really thought about where the glaistig's information came from. Like the shimmerlings' glow, the petals' sleeping pollen, she had just assumed Ciara *knew* secrets. Why hadn't Pip warned her?

"I knew we shouldn't have gone to the glaistig," Pip said.

"You said we shouldn't go because you were afraid we'd be eaten!" Jade said.

"That too!" Pip said. "Isn't being worried about being eaten enough?"

My dear child, think about it, Aron said, picking up a short, slender, ink-black flute with rubies inset along its length in a diamond pattern like a snake's skin. *If someone else had discovered me, wouldn't I have been stopped by now? Just because we are in the Feywild doesn't mean everything is magic. How did you think Ciara knew to look for you that night?*

The banshrae had planned it all out. This had all been an elaborate trap. Vira was right—the faeries had been manipulating her, she just wasn't right about which faeries, and not in the way she had been expecting.

Ciara's services are not cheap, Aron said, *as I'm sure you've found out, but well worth it in the end, I think. At least for the higher bidder.*

He'd been outside the room when she'd gone into the prince's chambers. He must have seen the locket glowing and figured out that the troves were there. He'd let Naomi go before the prince could talk to her—which Frost had later blamed her for. Aron had let Ciara know where Jade was so that when the "prophecy" came true, she'd go to the glaistig, to whom she would give the one valuable piece of information she had—the way to open the Ice Queen's trove. Aron knew that she had the password because she had had to go into the Ice Queen's trove to unfreeze Davin. And in return, she'd get the one piece of information she most craved—the identity of the person who was holding her sister, which Aron had so willingly supplied Ciara with, leading her straight into his trap.

"You're lucky I chose to ask who was holding my sister. There were a lot of other things I might have asked!" Jade said.

Because you'd ask where the troves were and end up here? Aron chucked. So the troves were still in the banshrae's room! He *had* stolen them! Not that she could do much about it now. *It was not much of a risk.*

She decided to change tactics. "What could the Ice Queen offer you when she was so cruel to you?" Jade asked.

"And how could you betray the Sun King, when he's done so much to help you?"

Done so much to help me? Like graciously allow me cook for all his endless, pointless feasts? Or, maybe, by restraining himself from mutilating me further? Aron snarled, waving the short black flute around. The flute made a whistling sound as it passed through the air. *The Sun King is weak. He has no power, and he is pinning his kingdom's only hope on a human girl, one who will inevitably end up a frozen sacrifice on the altar of the Ice Queen. Even without her trove, she has power enough to make winter encroach and to freeze those who stand against her! Don't you get it? You're working for the wrong side—the losing side. And you're going to end up just one more icicle in her garden of would-be heroes.*

Aron looked at the flute for a moment, then slapped it back on the wall with enough violence to cause all the other flutes to shake and make an eerie whistling sound. His fingers ran over the lengths of three more flutes—one carved of jade in the shape of a dragon, one of yew wood with inset moonstones, and one of burnished steel.

I am going to bring you to the Ice Queen, and then she shall have her trove, the password, the girl with the locket, and thus, access to her entire arsenal of winter magic. And it will all be because of me, Aron said.

No, Jade thought, it will all be because of me. Her heart was in her throat. I've messed it up. Again. Couldn't she

201

do anything right? Every time she thought she was ahead of the game, she was really behind and just couldn't see around the next bend.

I think that earns me back my mouth, Aron said. *Don't you?*

Of course! That was it! "I'm sure the Sun King and the Sun Prince could get you your mouth back!" Jade said quickly.

Don't you think I thought of that? They can't. Only the one who stole it can return it, Aron said. *And I wouldn't count on the Sun Prince for doing much of anything. He's a bit . . . tied up at the moment. No doubt his father is disappointed, but he is his mother's son in many ways, so willing to break the rules, even the scant few he's not allowed to.*

Now. If I may continue.

Aron's hand paused on a long, sinister-looking instrument: another flute, this one as white as bone, with swirling gray runes carved down its length that flashed iridescent as a pixie's wings in the light. He stroked its length and smiled down at it. Then he held it as though he were going to play—without breath, without lips. Vira, Pip, and Jade all stared at him as though he were crazy.

But just then a haunting song filled with all the loneliness she felt at being abandoned and forgotten on her birthday, all the despair she felt when she realized the Forever Court had pinned all the hopes on her—the wrong girl, who had no idea what to do, no one to help her, and no home to return to—rose up and filled the chamber.

How was he doing that? Jade thought. She was filled with sad and terrible wonder. Magic, again. What horrible magic.

She was so absorbed in the tragic melody that she failed to notice the effects of Aron's magic until Pip came barreling at her out of the air.

"Down!" Pip cried, pushing Jade aside. Two green darts, slender as needles, buried themselves in the frosting curtains by the window. A third pierced Pip's leg.

Pip's eyes rolled back in her head, and she fell to the ground like a rock.

"Pip, no!" Jade cried. The frosting where the darts had hit started dripping down the gingerbread walls. Why hadn't she thought to bring any of Quinn's silencing bombs? And why had Pip wasted hers on Vira? Sure, her sister was annoying, but she wasn't trying to kill them.

Grabbing one of Aron's other flutes off the wall, Vira dived behind the puff-pastry sofa. Vira was right. They couldn't just react, they had to act if they expected to get out of here! But Jade was out of tricks. No more silence bombs, no more stickyballs, no more trick ropes, and no more glitterbombs.

Jade glanced around for something she could use as a weapon. She wasn't a warrior! She was too small to fight on the banshrae's terms. What was she supposed to do? Bite him as if she were an insect?

Aron's tune picked up speed, and Jade watched as three more green darts materialized out of thin air and began circling his head like vultures. He blew out a series of three sharp notes, and the darts raced after Vira.

One buried itself in the couch, another in a butter cushion, and the third just missed her leg as she raced out from behind the couch and swung the flute as hard as she could across his midsection, causing him to fire his next three darts early and erratically into the ceiling.

But it seemed Aron was not just skilled at flute playing. He slipped the flute between Vira's legs and lunged to the side, pulling her off balance. Then he stood, shoving her up and back with the flute hooked under her knee so that she tumbled to the ground and lay there, sprawled on her back. Aron strode over to Vira and put his knee on her chest.

You interrupted me. Don't you know how rude it is to interrupt someone while they're playing? Aron said. He started to play again, summoning three more darts of green light.

"No!" cried Jade, flying up to his arm. Jade pulled at his sleeve and the darts flew into the chocolate flooring on either side of Vira, missing by mere inches. Vira scrambled to her feet. Aron casually dislodged Jade with a fling of his arm, sending her sailing into frosting.

Aron increased the tempo of his music, summoning four darts this time. Vira ran looking for another weapon, but the room was very small. She grabbed a butter pillow as a shield.

Like that would do much good, Jade thought in despair.

But then, just as Jade struggled free of the frosting, it gave her an idea. Scooping up a large handful of the sticky stuff, Jade flew over to Aron and stuffed frosting down the end of the flute. The music stopped, and the green darts faded.

Bothersome pixie! Aron snarled.

Jade soared away, but she wasn't quick enough. Covering all the flute's holes with his fingers, Aron blew one hard, sustained note, sending the frosting flying out like a missile and gluing Jade to the wall so that only her face and toes stuck out.

He resumed playing. The green darts materialized, and Jade was helpless to stop them.

"Jade Farstar!" Vira screamed, the spell of silence having finally worn off as she rushed the banshrae. Aron blew four short notes, and the darts flew at Vira. Jade watched in horror as they embedded themselves in her neck, all the way from her collarbone to right under her ear. Vira stopped in her tracks and her hand went up to feel where the darts were. Then, on wobbling feet, she took three more steps and fell at the banshrae's feet.

"Vira!"

The green glow drained out of the darts, and Jade could see it, still shining as it entered Vira's bloodstream.

Aron looked over at Jade. *As for you . . .* He did a quick trill, summoning up just one tiny dart, and sent it her way with an almost lazy puff of air. It hit her foot, and the world went black.

Chapter Twenty

When she came to, Jade Farstar was in a room carved out of ice fitted with a door made of rusting iron. There was only a very small window, covered in a thick sheet of ice, from which she could make out that it was not yet dawn. Good. It was not too late—yet, if the glaistig's prophecy could be believed, after all she had learned.

"Pip? Pip, where are you?" Jade asked, flying around the room. She looked down at her arms in disgust. She was still covered from head to toe in sticky, sugary dust from the frosting. Yuck. Gods, if you're listening, she thought, I promise never to eat dessert again if only you'll get me and my friends out of here safely!

"Pip!" But there was no sign of the pixie.

"She's not here," Vira said, sitting in the back corner of their small room, hugging her knees to her chest, watching Jade, her eyes haunted.

"Where is she?" Jade asked, a little embarrassed for not calling after Vira first. But Vira was always saying how she could take care of herself. "What have they done with her?"

"I don't know," Vira said. "She was gone when I woke up." Jade's heart fell.

"They better not have hurt her," Jade said, flying around the room anxiously. "Just because they're winter faeries and she's a summer faerie."

"Maybe she was on their side all along," Vira said darkly.

"Don't even say that!" Jade said. "She saved my life—several times over. She sacrificed herself for me when the banshrae's first darts flew. She helped me find you, against her own best interests. And she was my guide into the Feywild. I thought it was Golden Leaf at first—it looked exactly like it did in your stories."

"She could just be manipulating you! She's clearly listened to our stories. How else would she know the name 'Vira Wyvernsting'? And she did put the locket in the faerie box where we always said gifts from the faeries appeared."

"And what would that have gotten her?" Jade said. "She's a summer faerie. She'll freeze in the Winter Kingdom. Besides, she didn't betray me. I decided where we would go and what we would do—including sneaking into Aron's room to rescue you!"

"Did you?" Vira asked.

"Shut up!" Jade said, her voice thick. "She's my friend, and now she's in trouble!" And she couldn't hold back the tears any longer. Vira looked startled for a moment, and then she held out her hand.

"Look, I'm sorry, Jade . . . Farstar," Vira said, and Jade was slightly mollified by her use of her faerie name. "I didn't know she meant so much to you. I just don't know who to trust anymore. Those winter elves acted like my friends and then they captured me and brought me to the Ice Queen, you know," Vira continued. "She was furious. Apparently, I was supposed to have something that I didn't. Your locket, I suppose. Then Aron took me away and I spent the rest of my visit in that horrible cage. I wonder how it would have gone differently if I had had it."

"Either you would have died," Jade said grimly, "or the Ice Queen would now be in control of the Feywild."

"I see that now," Vira said. "Instead, I led her right to you."

"At least you didn't give the Ice Queen her trove back, filled with all the magic she'll need to defeat the Forever Court," Jade said.

"Her what?" Vira asked. "How in the world did you do that?"

"Her trove. It's a secret, magical room carved entirely of ice and filled with powerful, forbidden winter magic that you can access only through this magical mirror," Jade said miserably. "And I let them know how to use it in exchange for finding out who was holding you."

"You did that for me?" Vira asked in a small voice.

"Yes," Jade said. "Pretty dumb, huh?"

"No, I don't think that was dumb at all," Vira said. "I think that was fantastic." They sat in silence for a minute.

Footsteps sounded down the icy hall.

"Look, I know we don't have much time, but I want you to know that I'm sorry," Vira said.

"Vira, no . . ." Jade started.

"No, listen," Vira said. "We'll work this out. This is like Golden Leaf, right? The place I've been telling stories about since I was a kid. I needed this place—as do you. I want to help you save it. Let's adventure one last time as Jade and . . . Vira Wyvernsting. And we'll save it. Together."

"Thanks . . . Vira Wyvernsting," Jade said. And she flew down and hugged her sister around the neck. She knew Vira could be brave. Sometimes she just needed reminding.

The footsteps stopped right in front of their door, and they heard the clink and grind of a key being turned in the heavy iron lock. The door swung open, and they saw Aron with a guard of seven redcaps, each with a scythe in his hands. The banshrae held his white flute, and he had a long, jagged knife made of crystal at his belt. He was dressed in a very different livery now—the reds and golds were replaced with whites, blacks, and blues. His solid black eyes glinted at them emotionlessly.

If I'm not interrupting anything . . . Aron said, and Jade quickly let go of Vira Wyvernsting's neck, but Vira still glared out at the banshrae.

"That jerk. If I do one thing before I go, I want to get back at him," she whispered to Jade.

"He's all yours," Jade whispered back.

The queen will see you now, Aron said, gesturing with his flute. *If you try to run, I will put you out again and have you dragged to the queen's chamber.*

Then he gestured for the two sisters to take their place between the redcaps.

"If you can make a run for it, do it," Vira whispered. "I'm too big, but you . . ."

"Not a chance," Jade whispered back.

I have my eye on you, pixie, Aron said, keeping his flute pointed at her back. Jade rolled her eyes at Vira Wyvernsting. Like she'd have an opportunity to escape anyway.

Aron led them down the icy hallway and into an open courtyard. The moon was setting. It was only an hour or two before dawn. Their time was almost up. As scared as she had been about not knowing what to do, Jade Farstar was now more worried that she wouldn't have enough time to do everything that needed doing.

The courtyard was littered with frozen faeries and humans alike, some with expressions of shock on their faces, their bodies in the middle of running away or trying to dodge an invisible missile, and others with a sad look of resignation on their faces. And lounging on and among them were young white dragons. There had to be at least a dozen of them, each the size of a small pony, just like the ones from the forest that had been coating everything in ice. Just like the one Naomi had ridden that froze Davin.

Then it hit her—that's how the Ice Queen was doing it. She didn't have her power back any more than the Sun King did. She had convinced white dragons to use their breath weapon to emulate her powers and spread false winter, freezing her enemies. She made it appear as though she still had her power, to make the Sun King desperate, desperate enough to send the locket out into the world and start the prophecy that would end the war. Jade wished she could tell Frost!

Passing through all those dragons was eerie. It was like something out of one of Vira's stories. One raised its head and snorted out a frozen cloud as they approached the large silver and black wrought-iron gate made of metal twisted into the shapes of roses with outsized thorns—the same as on Frost's wand, she realized. Just then, Jade saw a familiar shape.

There, on a block of ice shorn from its original location was Phoenix, her fiery red hair, gold crown of metal flames glittering with gems, and her defiant, determined look all exactly the same as the last time Jade saw her.

Jade was sure it had been put there to intimidate her, or for the Ice Queen to see the evidence of her defeated enemies every morning, but Jade took strength from it. She put her fist to her heart in silent salute to the one who had gone before and now stood defiant—even in death—at the queen's gates for all eternity.

"Who's she?" Vira asked.

"Phoenix," Jade said. "The queen's daughter, who stood up to her and paid the price. A real hero."

"The queen froze her own daughter?" Vira said. "I'd hate to see what she does to her enemies! What have you gotten us into?"

"What have *I* gotten us into?" Jade smiled despite the circumstances. "Who started with the tales of Golden Leaf?"

"Ah, fair enough," Vira said, but now she was smiling too.

Before we go in, Aron said, *hold still.* And he gestured to the redcaps. The evil little old men crept up to the girls, rope in their hands, and started to tie their arms behind their backs. Vira struggled and Jade flew out of reach.

"What, is the Ice Queen afraid or something?" Jade cried, dogging the grabbing hands of the redcaps below.

We can always do this the hard way, Aron offered, waving his flute.

Vira Wyvernsting and Jade Farstar looked at each other. They were far less likely to escape those sleeping darts than a bit of rope. Jade flew down, and Vira stopped struggling. The redcaps roughly tied the girls' arms behind their backs—Vira with rope, Jade with twine—leaving a long tail like a kite on both Jade and Vira Wyvernsting. Jade turned her face away, trying not to smell their rotting breath, and immediately flew higher as soon as she was able. Flying with her arms tied back was as awkward as running over a carpet of marbles.

Aron tapped twice on the gates with the bone flute, and before he could tap a third time, they swung open, creaking on old and rusty hinges. The opening to a giant, icy cavern yawned before them like the throat of dragon and, almost as though it had taken a breath, Jade felt pulled inside.

"Come in, come in," said a cold, dead voice that echoed in the expanse of the chamber.

Vira took one step onto the icy floor, and without her arms for balance, almost fell. She looked at Aron incredulously.

"What happened since I was last here?" Vira said.

The Ice Queen was . . . displeased that you did not come with the locket she so desired, Aron said.

"I said, come in," snarled the voice. Jade felt herself being pulled through the air—and saw her sister pulled across the icy floor—past columns of ice and iron, past blue-flamed candelabras, past Aron and the redcaps, all the way into the Ice Queen's chambers, where Vira promptly fell, face first, without her arms to take the brunt of the fall. Jade spun out of control into a column and then, stunned, tumbled to the ground. When Vira managed to struggle to her feet, her nose was bloodied, and she had a scrape above her eye.

Jade shook her head and rose into the air. Her locket, she saw, was glowing again. Before her, the Ice Queen sat in a throne of twisted silver roses, black metal thorns, and crystal leaves encrusted in ice.

Curled around the base of the throne was the biggest of the white dragons—the size of a full-grown horse—its head in the Ice Queen's lap. She thought she recognized the puckered scar across its right eye from the dragon Naomi had ridden earlier—Rimewind. As though the Ice Queen could sense Jade thinking about her dragon, she reached down and stroked the icy, shimmering scales behind the frills on the white dragon's head. Rimewind half closed its eyes in contentment and began a soft rumble in its throat that sounded disturbingly like a cat's purring.

The Ice Queen herself had skin so white it sparkled like snow, and hair so dark it swallowed the light around her. Her lips, like her eyes, were as bright red as freshly spilled blood. A long, white gown with a dark sapphire lining wrapped her body from shoulders to ankles, and her feet were dressed in shoes with a pointy toe. In her right hand, she held a silver mirror–her trove. She appeared to be examining herself in it, though Jade knew that mirror did not reflect anything of this world.

"Vira Wyvernsting," the Ice Queen breathed, not looking up from the mirror. "We've met before. I was devastated when you failed me so soon into our acquaintanceship."

"But I–" Vira started.

"All is forgiven. Your presence, I'm sure, was instrumental in bringing me the locket," the Ice Queen said as though Vira Wyvernsting hadn't begun to talk at all. "Now, don't be rude. Introduce me to your sister."

"This is Jade Farstar–" Vira began, only to be cut off by the quiet but somehow dominating voice of the Ice Queen.

"Jade Farstar. Such a pretty name for such a pretty pixie," the Ice Queen said. "Jade Farstar, I think we got off on the wrong foot."

"If you call being hunted, nearly killed by redcaps, captured, and thrown in your prison 'getting off on the wrong foot,' then yes," Jade said, "we did."

"What was I supposed to do? The Sun King and my traitorous son had already poisoned your mind against me," the Ice Queen said, lowering her mirror to fix her cold gaze on Jade. "But we don't have to be enemies. I just need one thing from you, something that has always been and should always be mine, something that was stolen from me–my power."

"So you can conquer the Feywild and exterminate all the summer faeries?" Jade said. "Never!"

"What concern is it of yours what I do to those who have hurt me and mine?" the Ice Queen said. "If you help me, I can help you—return you to your natural shape, send you home, and you never have to worry about this strange, confusing world of faeries ever again."

"Some of those faeries are my friends!" Jade said. How could the Ice Queen even think she'd give them up?

"Are they? How many, exactly, would like you so well if they knew who you really are?" the Ice Queen said. "They are not your friends. This is not your fight. And you do not want to stand between me and my objectives. Phoenix stood between me and my goals, and because of that misunderstanding, she came to a most unfortunate end."

"Because you killed her, she came to a most unfortunate end," Jade said.

"But her fate does not have to be your own," the Ice Queen said. "Just help me—so that I can help you."

"Are you done yet?" Jade said.

"Yes," the Ice Queen replied, eyeing her pensively and stroking Rimewind's scales.

Jade held her face firm, determined not to show any signs of weakness. It would only take one—the gods knew the Ice Queen was testing her enough for them—and the queen would exploit it mercilessly. Jade liked to think she'd be strong enough to resist such an attack, but she didn't really even want to know.

"I'm not helping you," Jade said. "Even if I wanted to, I don't know how." That should shut her down. She couldn't do what she didn't know how to do, right?

"Ah, I can help you there," the Ice Queen said, her eyes glittering with hunger. She had found her opening. "You have the locket, and it is the key to opening the troves—it and the human girl who wears it. See how it responds to the trove? Glowing brighter when you get closer." Of course, Jade thought. That's why it glowed so brightly by the prince's wardrobe, and again in the banshrae's chambers! "It is linked with the trove. And my dear friend Aron has gotten me the password—the same one you used to open my trove for my son. All you have to do is place your hand on the locket, say the words I tell you, and I will be able to access it."

But what would happen to her sister, and to herself, if she granted the queen's wish? Jade had a feeling that was a one-way road to Phoenix's cell.

"Jade Farstar, no!" a strong, hard voice called out. Jade spun and saw Frost striding into the hall. Jade felt a warm rush. The Forever Court hadn't abandoned her. There was still hope.

"Who let him in?" the Ice Queen said, scanning the redcaps and banshrae with a dark look in her eyes.

"Don't do it," Frost said. Then, Jade was aware of something very hot right behind her.

"I wasn't going to," Jade said, annoyed. What did he think of her?

"Don't move," a familiar voice whispered in her ear, as Jade began to smell smoke. "I'm almost through these."

"Pip!" Jade breathed. "So that's where you ran off to. I thought you were a goner!"

"Not me!" Pip grinned. "I was just awake enough to hide after being hit with that dart, so I hid in the frosting. I knew you two would need help—a pair of humans against the Ice Queen? You didn't stand a chance. And Aron told me right where to find Frost—the only one likely to believe me. There. Done! I'm leaving just a thread attached on each so they don't fall and give away the game." Jade felt warmth flood into her arms as the ropes loosened. "I'm going over to do the same for your sister."

"She doesn't have a choice," the Ice Queen said without looking at Jade. "She wants to go home, doesn't she? And right now, she's all alone. She knows the risk she's taking."

"She's not alone," Frost said. "I'm here."

Jade felt a sudden rush. Maybe they could do this after all. Maybe they could defeat the Ice Queen.

"A touching sentiment. But I'm afraid that merely makes you what her sister already is—leverage," the Ice Queen said. "I will get what I want. That is inevitable. We are merely determining the matter of *how* I get what I want. Jade, if I were you, I'd make up my mind before I have to stop being so polite."

"I can't do that," Jade said.

"Jade Farstar, I am losing patience," the Ice Queen said. "Give me what I want, now, or I will freeze you, take the locket, and see if your sister is more reasonable."

"I would never help you," Vira said. "Not after the way you treated me."

"Is that so? And here I thought you might want to actually go home. Well, then," said the Ice Queen. "Give me what I want, or I let my pet dragon use your sister as target practice."

"Don't give in," Vira said. "You are not alone. We still have a chance." Jade could tell she was referring to the arrival of Pip and Frost and the cut ropes.

Jade hesitated. Did Vira mean for them to run now? If so, how would they defeat the Ice Queen? Vira was staring at her very intently. What was she trying to say?

"Is that your answer then?" the Ice Queen said.

"No, it's . . ." Jade began, still trying to puzzle out the meaning in Vira Wyvernsting's eyes.

"*Rimewind!*" the Ice Queen cried, pointing a long, bony finger at Vira Wyvernsting. The white dragon curled around the queen's throne raised its head and took in a deep, rasping breath.

"Mother, no!" the Sun Prince said, leaping in front of the blast and knocking Vira out of the way. Vira tumbled to the ground, a scream of pain leaving her lips as her head hit the ice again, her arms still bound behind her back. Jade thought she could hear Pip cursing. A bright, tightly controlled stream of white light shot out from Rimewind's jaws and blossomed into ice, wrapping around Frost's feet and holding him solidly to the ground. All was silent for a moment, and then the prince gasped in shock.

"Oh no," said Jade. She felt her heart drop into her stomach.

"My son, sacrificing yourself for a human," the Ice Queen said while gesturing for Rimewind to continue to coat the prince in ice. Frost struggled, but the white dragon effortlessly exhaled more ice, this time around his calves. "And I had such high hopes for you."

"Sorry to disappoint you, Mother," Frost said, grimacing as the ice extended another inch over his knees.

"You know, I think you killed the last warm part of me with your betrayal," the Ice Queen said as Rimewind coaxed ice up his thighs. The prince's breath had turned frosty and was staining the air white. "You were my last bit of summer."

"Then set me free," Frost urged, his lips blue and his teeth chattering. "Teach me, mold me, but what good does it do to freeze me into another one of your endless ice sculptures to decorate your garden?"

"I will have you at home, the perfect sculpture of a good son, right next to my perfect sculpture of a good daughter. What more could a mother want?" the Ice Queen said. "Perhaps the sight of it will warm my heart."

"What heart is that?" Frost said. "The heart that refused to let the Forever Court have its rightful domain? The heart that froze your own daughter? The heart that litters your garden with innocents?" The ice was up to his waist now, and the prince's face was contorted in pain. Rimewind showed no signs of slowing. "You don't have a heart!"

"And that is why you I do not set you free," the Ice Queen said. "The Sun King's blood runs strong in you." The Ice Queen smiled at him frostily as the ice crept up his chest. "Perhaps when you are older"—the queen turned her head away and resumed examining her trove, as though refusing to see the end result of her command—"and more prone to listening to reason, we can talk about your release."

"Mother!" Frost yelled. "Don't turn your back on me!"

Jade flew over to him and whispered, "Stop struggling." She could feel the cold radiating off of the icy cage. "Rimewind only freezes you faster when you struggle."

"He's your own son!" Vira said from the ground, blood staining her face and the ice around her. "How can you do that to your own son?"

"I know. Tragic, isn't it? He was to be my successor," the Ice Queen said. "Now, Jade, you are going to open my trove for me unless you want your sister to suffer the same fate. Rimewind will not miss a second time."

This was what must have happened to Phoenix. Jade had thought Phoenix must have been frozen instantaneously, like Davin. What a cold heart a mother must have to use a dragon to freeze her children bit by bit while they still have breath to cry out for mercy. Jade tried to imagine standing still, defiant as Phoenix had been, staring down the Ice Queen as the ice crept up her body, sealing her in for all time.

"Don't give up yet," Vira whispered. " 'White dragons are notoriously dumb.' "

It took a moment for what Vira said to sink in. And then, it hit her. The stories from Golden Leaf. The trap with the white dragon. But she didn't see anything that looked like a place she could create a cave-in, and she didn't have the means to do so, anyway. In fact, the only thing she saw similar between the two scenarios at all was the white dragon. What did they have that was like the ice trap? What was like a cave-in?

Then, as though she could read Vira Wyvernsting's thoughts, she saw what her sister meant—and it sunk it. It was unbelievably risky—dangerous as dancing with a hungry bullette—but it might actually work. She nodded, very slightly, to her sister in understanding. Now, to pretend that she was lost and confused—trapped. As though that required much work.

"Jade Farstar," the Ice Queen said, her fingernails drilling the arms of her throne with impatience.

"All right!" Jade said, looking Vira straight in the eyes. "All right. Don't hurt her. I'll do it."

The Ice Queen smiled without warmth. "I'm so glad we could work this out," she said.

"Jade Farstar, don't!" Frost said. "Whatever she's promised you, she lies. She'll just freeze the two of you as soon as she has her power again. You know it's true."

"I never lie, unlike some relatives I could mention. Now, Aron"—the Ice Queen kept her eyes locked on Jade as she held out her hand imperiously—"the password."

Ah, of course. Just a moment, Aron said as he began to rifle through the pouch at his belt.

"The password!" Frost groaned. "How in the world did she find that out? You and I were the only ones who knew it."

"Er . . ." Jade mumbled, looking down. "Sorry about that."

"You fool!" Frost said. "No wonder the prophecy suggests your sister."

"You be quiet!" Jade said. "I'm doing the best I can!"

"Yes, well, your best just isn't good enough," Frost said. "You've compromised or ruined everything we've worked for, all trying to 'help.' You can stop trying to help any time you like!" The ice climbed up to his shoulders. Rimewind seemed to be enjoying the slow torture, but the dragon also seemed to take longer in between sessions now, as though it were getting tired.

"Like you were around to help her!" Pip whispered angrily.

"Leave her alone," Vira said. "She's fought for you more than you know, and you want to criticize her for not being me? I would have abandoned you long before now."

Jade felt a flush at Vira Wyvernsting's compliments and turned to her sister, but her sister was glaring at the Sun Prince. Frost looked like he was about to answer, but Aron had found the password scrawled on a bit of parchment.

My queen, Aron said, bowing and holding it up in offering. *The password.* Frost glared at Jade.

"You fool," Frost said. "You really did it. You gave up the only secret you had to keep, that you weren't even supposed to have in the first place."

Jade focused on looking at everything but the Sun Prince.

"Ah, thank you, Aron," the Ice Queen said. "You truly have been a loyal servant." She placed a hand on his forehead and the banshrae stood very still and closed his eyes, as though he expected some magic or the other. Then she plucked the parchment out of his hands.

"Free Jade's arms," the Ice Queen said.

My queen? Aron asked, opening his eyes.

"Do it," the Ice Queen said without looking at him. Pulling his flute off his back, Aron looked at Jade with murder in his eyes. Jade held her breath, expecting the worse, but he just blew a trill on his flute and sent a green dart through the remaining threads holding her arms behind her back. Smoke drifted up from the frayed ropes, Aron snapped the flute on his back again, and she was free. For half a second, she thought about fleeing, or fighting, or something, but then the Ice Queen interrupted her train of thought.

"Now, Jade," the Ice Queen said, ignoring the expectant banshrae, "place your hand on the locket." Jade brought her fingers to hover over the locket and chanced a look at Vira Wyvernsting. Vira bit her lip, but nodded.

Jade let her fingers touch the locket, and immediately, the radiant glow around it grew bright as the sun and spread to the Ice Queen's mirror. Both the mirror and the locket began pulsing in time with her heart. The room grew warmer, a small circle of ice on the floor melted in a halo around her, and flowers began pushing their heads through the ground, filling the room with scents of daffodils, buttercups, and daisies.

"This is the end, you know," Frost said to Jade, but he was helpless to stop her, encased in ice up to his shoulders.

"This is how the war ends, with you betraying the Forever Court."

"Now, repeat after me," the Ice Queen said, glancing at the parchment. "*Alrhys rahv iislira.*"

Jade hesitated, looking at the deep grief and fury written on the prince's face. She closed her eyes so she wouldn't have to see it, and took a deep breath, hoping they knew what they were doing.

"I'm sorry, Your Highness, but I have to do this," Jade said.

"Why?" he said, echoing her nightmare in the forest. But in the forest, she didn't have an answer. Here, she had a plan. At least she hoped she had a plan.

"*Alrhys rahv iislira.*"

The moment the last word left Jade's lips, her locket flashed, and the silver skin of the mirror began to writhe like so many snakes. It was open.

The Ice Queen laughed. It was an awful sound, like the shattering of glass. Jade flew backward a bit, and Vira scrambled a few steps back as well. Then the Ice Queen stood, flush with her recent victory, and held the mirror out.

"My magic! My crown, my necklace, my jewels, my wand . . . how I have missed the feel of their power," the Ice Queen said. She turned to Rimewind. "I am going into my trove now. I will not wait another minute before reclaiming what is mine. The Forever Court will tremble before me once again. Rimewind, find Naomi. You two will prepare the white dragons and the winter faeries for war! We ride at dawn."

Rimewind bowed, touching its jaws to her feet, and the queen graced the dragon's shoulders with her touch. Then the dragon raced out of the throne room, unfurling its wings for flight.

The Ice Queen watched Rimewind go for a moment, and then she hooked the mirror into a spot on the head of her throne. The mirror fit right into the spot as though it were made for it, nestled among the iron roses like a great silver eye. Then she brought her fingers to the now liquid metal surface. The corners of her lips turned up in what Jade couldn't quite bring herself to call a smile.

What have I done? Jade thought. This had better work, or I have doomed the Feywild far worse than had I simply failed to defeat her.

My queen, Aron said. *The prisoners!*

"Yes?" the Ice Queen asked. "What about them?"

What should I do with them? Aron asked.

"Watch them, fool," the Ice Queen said. "A pixie, an ice sculpture, and a human girl, all restrained. On the odd chance that you should somehow fail to keep order and they do manage some mischief, I will feed your mouth to my redcaps. Is that incentive enough?"

Yes, your majesty, Aron said, bowing deeply again.

"Good. See that you are here when I return," the Ice Queen said, and she pressed her fingers into the mirror and disappeared. Frost watched her pass through with a sick look plastered across his face.

"What a grateful queen you have there," Jade said, catching Vira Wyvernsting's eye and giving her a silent countdown with her fingers behind her back. "She sure sounds like someone who is going to give you back your mouth and a kingdom to boot."

Aron spun around to face her. *Bothersome pixie!* he snarled, swiping at her.

"Now!" called Jade, bursting free from her ropes and dodging Aron's hands.

The banshrae looked confused, but by the time he turned around, Vira had already burst her ropes and was running full speed at Aron, yelling an angry, very human battle cry. Her shoulder impacted his gut, and she tackled him to the ground. They both went sliding across the icy floor. Aron's head smashed into a column, and he stopped struggling for just an instant. That was long enough for Vira to climb on top of him and pin his arms to his sides.

"Jade Farstar, catch!" Pip yelled, and she threw Jade one of the knapsacks filled to bursting with all manner of pixie tricks. Jade caught it and swung it over her shoulder.

"Thanks!" Jade said, turning to face the stunned redcaps. And, side by side, Jade and Pip flew at the redcaps, dive bombing them and pelting them with stickyballs, glitter-bombs, and pixie rope traps.

Three redcaps raced at Jade. She dodged, diving between them, narrowly missing getting her wings clipped by one scythe and just escaping the closing grip of another, as she aimed her stickyballs at the soles of their feet.

When she finished with her three, she looked up to see that Pip's redcaps were bound in the trick ropes and bouncing around on the floor like fish out of water. Jade couldn't help but laugh as they skated unintentionally across the icy floor.

"Jade Farstar, behind you!" Frost said. "Your sister!"

Jade whipped around just in time to see Aron buck Vira off, sending her sliding across the room. He climbed unsteadily to his feet, his black eyes filled with hate, and focused on Jade.

That's about enough of that, he said, pulling his flute from his back.

"Oh no you don't," Jade said. "Not this time!"

Aron played three notes and the green darts started to materialize, but then Jade and Pip both threw smoke-filled glass balls at the banshrae, one hitting him and the other hitting his flute. Aron's flute suddenly went silent, the end twisting into a pixie knot, and the green darts disappeared. He threw away the flute, sending it skittering after Vira Wyvernsting, and reached for the knife—that wasn't there.

"Looking for this?" Pip smirked, pulling the crystal knife from her magical haversack. Then Jade threw another ball at him, this one a glitterbomb, blinding him just as Vira came charging at him from behind, holding his flute like a bat. This time, instead of hitting him in the stomach, she clubbed him on the back of his head, and he fell, motionless but still breathing, to the ground. Vira raised the flute, ready to club him again should he stand up, but he stayed down, unconscious.

"The mirror!" Jade said as Vira surveyed the fallen banshrae. "Quick, before he wakes up or she comes back!"

"Right," said Vira Wyvernsting, and she switched the flute so that she held one end of it, then sent it sailing, end over end, as hard and fast as an arrow from a bow. It hit the exact center of the mirror. There was a tremendous crackling sound, like thunder. And then cracks blossomed out from the center of the mirror like a spiderweb. The glass shattered and fell the ground, leaving blank, black wood in its place in the mirror's frame.

In the broken pieces that lay on the ground, Jade could see the Ice Queen throw herself at the other side of the mirror, her teeth bared, and every vestige of humanity and nobility gone, replaced with rabid, animal fury. But it was a soundless, ineffective fury, almost as though she had been hit with one of Quinn's silent bombs. And although Jade flinched when the Ice Queen made impact with the other side of the mirror, the queen was unable to affect anything on the other side of the mirror. She was trapped.

"We did it, we did it, we did it!" Pip shouted.

"Way to go, Jade Farstar!" Vira cried.

Pip and Jade flew over to Vira, and the three exchanged smiles of celebration.

"Who'd have thought that plan would actually have worked!" Jade said. "I mean, it worked in your stories, but this is the real world!"

"Yeah," Vira said. "Wouldn't it have been awful if it had failed? But what choice did we have?"

"So you did have a plan," Frost said from inside his icy cocoon. His lips had turned blue enough to match his eyes, Jade noticed, her heart sinking. They hadn't won every battle. "You had me worried there for a minute. I thought you were just making it up as you went along."

"So did I, you know, for a minute there," Jade said.

Frost laughed, a somewhat forced sound from his constricted lungs.

"And you must be the real Vira Wyvernsting," Frost said, addressing Vira. "It is good to have you here as well. Without your help, we could never have defeated the Ice Queen."

"It's an honor," Vira said, slightly choked up.

"You weren't supposed to do this alone, you know," Frost said to Jade. "We were supposed to go together."

"It's not like you left me much of a choice," Jade said,

looking at him sadly. While she might go home, Frost would not be so lucky. Did there always have to be a sacrifice for good to triumph? Was it impossible to have a truly happy ending? She was not looking forward to telling the Sun King what had happened to his son.

"Still, I am glad to see that your heart is in the right place and that I got to live to see it," Frost said. "I would not want to die thinking of you as a traitor when you have done so much for us."

"Now hold on, no one's saying good-bye," Jade said, surprised to find herself sniffling. "You're not dead yet."

"No, it's too late," Frost said. "You destroyed the Ice Queen's trove. Where else will you find the power? Tell my father . . . tell him I'm sorry."

"Tell him yourself!" Jade said.

"You know I'm not coming back," Frost said. "It's all I deserve. It took a couple of pixies and a human girl to show me the way before I had the bravery Phoenix had all those years ago."

"No," Jade started.

"Hey," Pip said. "Didn't the banshrae steal *both* troves?"

"You know, Pip," Jade said, a smile starting to spread across her face as she realized what Pip meant to do. "I believe he did."

"Are you thinking what I'm thinking?" Pip said, a mischievous smile on her face.

Chapter Twenty-One

They arrived at the Forever Court on the backs of winged horses the Sun Prince had called with a silver whistle, just as the sun peeked over the horizon. That in itself was an adventure. For one thing, Jade was awake to see their flight over the Ice Queen's lands this time. For another, she had always wanted to ride on the back of a flying horse!

It didn't seem real—that the war could really be over, that they could really have defeated the Ice Queen, that everyone could really be all right and able to go home again—until Jade saw the snow white walls of the Forever Court painted in shades of dawn and surrounded by its endless gardens. The Sun King and his faerie court were all arrayed before the wrought gold gates, and they had banners, each with a yellow sunburst on a crimson field. But something was wrong. Instead of having their arms open in welcome, they held their swords drawn and were dressed in the finely woven steel shirts they wore to battle.

"Halt, traitors, in the name of the Sun King!" said one of the elves in the lead.

"What is the meaning of this?" the Sun Prince said. "Don't you know who I am?"

"Yes, they do," a mellow, deep voice said. As the Sun King made his way up, his guards parted like water. "When you escaped from your chambers, leaving your guards covered in glue and glitter and sound asleep, and the Ice Queen's dragons of war sounded at the setting of the moon, I had no choice but to fear the worst."

Jade suddenly found that she was furious. Did the Sun King even know how close he'd come to losing his only son? Hadn't Frost suffered enough? And as though the Sun King had done anything to help defeat the Ice Queen! Adults were so unfair when they judged their children. She wished they held themselves to the same draconian standards.

"Leave him alone," Jade said. The Sun King's eyebrows rose, and he examined her closely. She hovered defiantly.

"Why should I?" the Sun King said. "He has broken the law—several laws, in fact."

"Because he just saved all of us by defeating the Ice Queen!" Jade said.

"Did he now?" the Sun King said, crossing his arms and looking down his nose at her. "And why should I believe you . . . pixie?"

"Because he also saved me," a new voice said, strong and clear. A gasp rang out across the collected faeries. A satyr swooned. The corners of Phoenix's lips twitched into a smile and she strode forward, her red hair flying behind her like a banner. "Well met, Father."

"Phoenix!" the Sun King said, his voice choked and his arms falling limp by his sides. "Is that really you?"

"Father, it's good to be home!" The Sun Princess threw protocol behind her and dashed across the ground to her father, who threw his arms open to receive her. "I have so much to tell you."

"I . . . I thought I'd lost you . . ." the Sun King said softly.

"You almost did. If it weren't for Jade Farstar, Vira Wyvernsting, Pip, and my brother, you would have," Phoenix said, pointing them out in turn.

"You're Jade Farstar?" the Sun King said, confusion crossing his face. "But I thought you were Vira Wyvernsting." Then he shook his head, smiling. "I can tell you have a long story to tell me. But that can wait. First"—he turned to Phoenix and embraced her with a gentleness Jade had not seen in the leonine king until then, and Phoenix returned the embrace with a joyful ferocity—"Welcome home." After a moment, the Sun King raised his gaze, his eyes wet but intensely happy and filled with pride. "All of you."

A cheer went up from the faeries, and Jade couldn't help but grin at the sight of the family, reunited at last. It made her think of her own family, and she was struck with a pang of homesickness. But then, Pip was hugging her, and Jade forgot again and was just happy in the moment.

"We can talk about the prophecy and your adventures later," the Sun King said after the cheering died down. "But for now, I believe a celebration is in order. The Ice Queen is defeated and my daughter is returned from the ice. The Sun Prince and Princess, Jade Farstar, Vira Wyvernsting, and the pixie Pip are the heroes of the day. And we are safe at long last. Let the music play, the food flow, and the dancing go all night!"

And then the cheering rose up again, and this time, it did not die down as they were all swept away into the Forever Court, all swords and armor forgotten.

"We really ought to get home," Vira said in a low voice. "Our mother is going to be really worried."

"We've been gone for three days," Jade said, caught up in the excitement. "We can be gone for a few more hours. You really have to experience at least one fun side of the Feywild before we go home—and I can't think of anything better for that than a party thrown in our honor!"

"All right," Vira conceded. "But only for a few hours."

But the hours passed like moments. They told the story of their adventure at least a hundred times, and how they had revived Frost and Phoenix using a combination of summer and winter magic from the Sun King's trove and the Ice Queen's wand, which luckily Frost had never returned to the Ice Queen's trove. Vira learned the Dance of the Twelve Sisters and played a song on the fiddle with the faerie band. Jade found out the recipe for the delicious sunny apples and took a turn around the dance floor with Quinn; and pixies were official, honored guests of the Forever Court. The sun had fully risen before Vira or Jade noticed the time.

"We have to get home," Vira said. And this time, Jade agreed. Making their way through the revelry to where Frost and Phoenix sat talking to the Sun King at the head of the room, they made their regrets to the king. The Sun King explained how Jade would change back into a human as soon as she crossed over into the mortal world again, and then told her how to activate the locket to take her and her sister home. Then the four of them made their way out to the same patio Jade had wandered out onto before by mistake when she met the glaistig.

"Do you understand?" the Sun King asked.

"Yes," Jade said. "Perfectly."

"Good. Take care. I know we haven't seen the last of you, Jade."

She bowed to the Sun King, and he inclined his head, smiling, and retreated to the doorway, leaving Frost and Phoenix to say their good-byes.

"Thank you for finishing what I started," Phoenix said.

"You were so brave to start it," Jade said.

"It's easy to be brave when you can't see the danger," Phoenix said. "It takes a lot of guts to go in fully knowing the dangers."

"Um, thanks," Jade said, blushing. She really wished she'd had longer to get to know the fiery Sun Princess.

"Until we meet again," Phoenix said, giving them each a quick salute and retreating to stand by the Sun King. That left Frost, who stood staring at Vira and Jade, with a strange expression on his face.

"Thank you for—" Frost and Jade started at the same time.

"You first," Frost said.

"What will happen to the winter lands and all the winter faeries?" Jade asked.

"As of tonight at sunset, I will no longer be the Sun Prince," Frost said sadly. Jade looked at him without understanding. Had the Sun King really gone and punished him after all he'd done for the Forever Court? After he'd helped them rescue Phoenix? That was going too far.

"What? He didn't dare," Jade said hotly. "You just wait here. I'll go talk to your father and . . ." What was that sound? She looked over and noticed Frost was laughing. Why was he laughing? This was serious!

"You misunderstand me," Frost said. "Phoenix has had enough of ice to last her a lifetime and has chosen to resume her duties as Sun Princess rather than take the winter throne. With no one to sit on the winter throne, I must return to my mother's land and claim her crown to become the Ice King."

"Oh no," Vira said. "That's awful."

"It's awful only if you're my mother," Frost said wryly. "I plan on being a very different kind of monarch."

"If you say so," Vira said dubiously. She did not look like she could be convinced that this was good news.

"Trust me," Frost said, smiling. "Farewell, Jade Farstar, Vira Wyvernsting."

"Good-bye," Vira said.

"You know you aren't half bad," Jade said. "I wished I'd gotten to know you earlier."

"Me too," said Frost.

"Jade Farstar!" Pip said, barreling through the air and into Jade with a flying bear hug, sending the two cartwheeling through the sky. "What do you mean by trying to sneak out and leave without saying good-bye?"

"Sneak out? Never," Jade said, grinning.

"Don't you forget about me, all right?" Pip said, sniffling.

"Forget about you?" Jade said. "How could I?"

"I'm serious!" Pip said, punching Jade in the shoulder. "Keep in touch through the faerie box. It's a portal of sorts to our world. You have to promise you'll write me."

"I will," Jade said. "I promise."

"All right," Pip said, letting go of her. "Then I guess you can go."

"Thanks for everything, Pip," Jade said. "You were the best Faerie Guide ever."

Taking one last look around her, Jade flew over to Vira, who held Jade's human clothes, and grabbed hold of her finger.

"Ready?" Jade asked, taking one last look around. The Sun King stood in the doorway, Frost and Phoenix by his side, waving. Pip hovered, looking on miserably nearby. The light from the party shined through the large castle windows. Laughter and fiddle music floated on the breeze. Was *she* ready? She was going to miss this place.

"Ready," Vira said. Too late for second-guesses now. Jade knew where she belonged. Home. Where her mother was waiting.

"*Araethi lythirae qiri,*" Jade whispered. The locket fell open like a storybook. Inside was engraved a perfect picture of their tree house, every detail perfect, down to the faerie box covered in leaves. Each carved line shimmered green and gold, and it was getting brighter every moment. And then, just as before, on her birthday, the world stopped. With an explosion of gold and green sparks, everything disappeared.

When they could see again, they were in the tree house at the edge of the forest by their home. Just by the size of the walls around her, Jade could tell she was a human again.

She shed the pixie garment–which had grown with her, surprisingly–and donned her human clothes. She folded up her pixie garment and hid it behind the faerie box. She would miss her wings, but she couldn't deny it felt good to be in her familiar form again. It was evening, and she could hear her mother calling.

"Vira? Jade? It's time for dinner!"

Jade and Vira looked at each other. That didn't sound very panicked. Had this all been a dream after all? Jade's hand went up to her chest–her locket was still there, closed. No, it had been real, all right. Vira appeared to be having similar thoughts.

"What's going on?" Vira asked. "She sounds like we've only been gone a few hours–but it's been days!"

Then something that Vira said triggered a memory of a passage in *A Practical Guide to Faeries*.

"I remember now," Jade said. "Time in the Feywild sometimes travels differently than it does in our world."

"You really were more cut out for this than me," Vira said, chuckling. "You have a perfect memory for anything that has to do with faeries."

"Yeah, well, it's your fault I'm interested in them to begin with," Jade shot back. "Come on, we don't want to be late for dinner!"

Jade tucked the locket inside her shirt, and then both girls scrambled down the tree and raced home. Jade could smell the warm baked bread, the savory roasted meat, and a sweet, lemony-chocolaty smell that could only be coming from her birthday cake. And she had thought she was going to miss her birthday entirely!

"There you are," her mother said. "I was beginning to get worried! Your birthday dinner is going to get cold."

"My birthday dinner . . ." Jade said.

"Yes, your birthday dinner," her mother said. "Did you think we'd forgotten? Oh, Vira! What happened to your face—and your hair?"

Jade looked over and noticed Vira still had a bit of crusted blood under her nose, and her forehead was still scraped up from her battle with the Ice Queen. And that white streak . . . that wasn't going away. Jade and Vira looked at each other and came to a silent accord.

"Nothing much," Vira said, sharing a smile with Jade. "Just playing."

"Really," her mother said, looking from one to the other in disbelief. "Just playing."

"Yes, really," Jade said. "Just playing. You worry too much, Mom!"

"Well, all right," her mother said. "If you two are going to be mum about it. Just don't play so rough next time."

"Yes, Mom," the girls said. And then, they sat down to the birthday evening Jade had been positive she wasn't going to get. It was perfect. Singing, dancing, drinking hot chocolate, and playing games. It wasn't a faerie party, but it was perfect, especially the part where Vira was extra nice to her. She supposed it had something to do with saving her life and all that. But Vira had been pretty brave herself. And it was exactly what Jade needed.

After the celebration ended, Jade went to bed and lay on her back in her lower bunk with the sheets pulled low like it was a cave. The food didn't taste half as good as faerie food—as *A Practical Guide to Faeries* had warned her it wouldn't—but that was all right, because she had had the most amazing adventure, and that was worth it.

That reminded her: she'd promised never to eat dessert again if the gods saw her out of that pickle alive. Well, hopefully they hadn't taken her seriously. Who really gave up dessert forever? They had to know that was an exaggeration. Or maybe she'd only given up dessert in the Feywild. But what in the world would she eat if she couldn't eat dessert in the Feywild?

She thought of all the sweets at their celebration in the Feywild—really, what else had there been to eat?—and of the Sun King's parting words to her as he'd led her out of the castle.

"Visit any time you like," he had said. "The locket is yours to keep now, and you are a hero of the Forever Court. When you're in the tree house, just whisper the words I taught you, and the locket will open and bring you here, where you will take on the form of a pixie once again. The same words will take you back home, but only after one full day in the Feywild. Do you understand?"

"Yes," she had said. "Perfectly."

"Good. Take care."

She put her hand on her locket. It was still warm.

"I know we haven't seen the last of you, Jade Farstar," the Sun King had said.

No, she thought as she closed her eyes. You most certainly haven't.

Acknowledgments

Thank you to my sister, Rachel, and my cousin, Erika, the original audience of my Golden Leaf stories, back when we were all kids. And thank you to Nina Hess, my editor, for all her encouragement, inspiration, and for her excellent eye for story and character.

About the Author

When **Susan J. Morris** was a child, she used to tell her sister stories about a place called Golden Leaf—a forest made of silver and gold where faeries dwell. When she got older, she became a fantasy editor, author, and game designer, writing *A Practical Guide to Faeries*, *A Practical Guide to Wizardry*, and *A Practical Guide to Dragon Magic*, and designing a kids' version of Dungeons & Dragons called Monster Slayers: Heroes of Hesiod. *The Faerie Locket* is her first novel. You can find her online at www.SeriousPixie.com.